NAN I THINK I'M BI

NAN I THINK I'M BI

Hilarious Anecdotes of the Bisexual and Bicurious

Thomasin Lockwood

Published by Vulpine Press in the United Kingdom in 2023

Illustrations by Thomasin Lockwood
Graphic rendering by Luka Hays

ISBN: 978-1-83919-545-7

www.vulpine-press.com

Dedicated to the people of Narnia who are sadly still trapped in the closet.

INTRODUCTION

Okay, okay, okay, so I've got some shit to get out of the way before I start telling you all my secrets. I'll try to be quick, but I just want to explain a little bit about why I decided to write this thing before we get into the gossip.

First of all: YOU. How did you get your hands on me, then? Did you buy me yourself? Was I a bargain on the Kindle? In the charity shop? At the airport? Or were you gifted me as a joke present by a well-meaning friend? Maybe I personally waved it in your face and begged you to buy it.

I'm not sure who you are, dear reader, and why you're feeling curious about the bicurious – or feeling sexual about the bisexual. But welcome. You may be accustomed with the issues or not, but I'd like to start the book by laying out the problem (generally speaking) that I've found in my interviews.

For bisexual women, I think sometimes our bisexuality is seen as something performative or explorative. A moot point. It's waved off as something that all women have at the very least *considered*, nothing to make a big deal out of here. Who *hasn't* drunkenly snogged their mate on a night out?!

1

A lot of the media I grew up with was framed by men, and I knew very early on that what hetero men loved more than having sex with a woman was having sex with many of them. Threesomes were joked and fantasised about, and the default was always two women lezzing out together and the guy also getting his fill. The ultimate experience! Meanwhile, a threesome with two men and a woman was referred to as *the Devil's three-way*. Yikes. Growing up, when I told (some) guys (and I MEAN some, not ALL but enough for me to notice a pattern okay?) that I thought I might be bisexual, it was, "Don't worry, we find it hot" or an uncomfortable, "Oh" as if I was inviting them to a threesome then and there. One homophobic guy I worked with told me, "You should really reconsider that." And if I told (some) girls it was usually met with a high-pitched, trying-to-be-normal, "oh right" and even occasionally a sceptical, "have you been with a girl? Then no you're not." Stop looking for attention. Worse still, I've seen some people theorise that bisexuality in women is a trauma response to abuse from a man. We don't have the time or know-how to unpack that here (are you laughing yet?) but it's another example of how bisexual women are being framed in a negative light. As if it's not an organic part of who they were 'meant' to be.

For bisexual guys, strangely it can be the opposite problem. I've always found that men's gender identity is so much more intertwined with their sexuality than women (see incels). They can't just say, "Nuts to the dating scene, I'm gonna start knitting and get a cat." I'm not saying women don't get shit for that, but their identity isn't called into question in the same way as it is for a man. It's rough. Bisexual men, as a result, can feel emasculated. They're less of a 'man'. They're dangerous. They're weird. I once slept with a guy that was so straight, when we were fooling around and he realised he had nerves in his ass and was very receptive to it, his first reaction was, "Oh god I shouldn't like that, but *I do*." *Why not?!* I thought, bamboozled. I, a grownup woman, was there and not a man. He'd had a religious upbringing and explained to me that for him, ass pleasure = gay sex! And gay sex! = BAD. It's all rather silly[1], really. So, for a bicurious man to go one step further and actually experiment with their own gender is like a land of no return, never mind how normal it was for the Spartans, some of the most kick-ass manly men that exist in our minds today. (Next time you're being accused of being bi in some kind of derogatory way, just say, "It's not gay, it's Spartan.") I really sympathize with the internal and external shame bi men can feel, from women desexualising them, to straight men feeling uncomfortable, to male love interests challenging them to stop beating around the bush and come out as a proud gay man. Bisexual men are out there, and they're not talking to you about it.

---

[1] Homophobic.

3

And then there are the non-binaries or trans people who are bisexual, who may face a two-for-one deal in terms of the issues already laid out, alongside trying to be accepted for the nuances of their own non-binary identity. Oof. Did I mention this book was meant to be a light-hearted read? Are you having fun yet, dear reader?

Like I say, this is all generally speaking. Many people are accepting and understanding of bisexuals. *Many people do not give a flying fuck.* Hooray! It's certainly going in the right direction. But I don't feel there's much representation of bi-sexuals in the media, and when there is it's often overly sex-ualised. The character usually has poor morals, is a bit of a mess or is even the villain (gay coding in villains is nothing new). But the worst part of it is that they're all just: *Way. Too. Cool.* I could deal with the poor morals, but seeing a bisexual who is smooth talking, sexy and sure of themselves seems so far off to me on my current journey. I guess that's the endgame? Sexy villain? A successful and fulfilled bisexual is like one of those cats that people have trained to use a human toilet. It's impressive, but there's probably been a lot of shit to deal with on the way.

Now see here, I'd like to note that I am fully aware that the literally life-threatening homophobia that lesbians and gay men can face is a much bigger issue than 'wahhh bisex-uals are all being portrayed as sluts or frauds!' I get that. Fur-thermore, my identity is a privilege. I am a white, (sort of) middle-class Brit who has had many opportunities in life

4

that I didn't earn. I'm sure if a witness at the Stonewall riots were to meet me, they'd very kindly (or curtly) tell me to get over my cheap self and stop overthinking this bi thing. Actually, it probably wouldn't even take a witness from that milestone of an event to reach that conclusion. My sexual identity is never going to be life and death like it is for so many other people in the LGBTQ community. At least I hope not. This book isn't here to unearth the turmoil of what it has taken for people to feel pride in oneself when homosexuality is still outlawed in many countries and the suicide rates in the trans community are so high. I am in no way qualified to cover that.

But what this book *can* do is to tell anyone who is bisexual or even bicurious that THERE IS NOTHING WRONG WITH YOU. And I think laughing about the pitfalls of exploring a sexuality that's either alien to you or unacceptable to others means we can better still celebrate the triumphs. Look at what the TV show *The Inbetweeners* did for cis male heterosexuality! It leaned into the awkwardness of it all and probably helped a load of horny, confused teenage boys feel a lot less alone (citation needed). Because bisexuality is an unsteady sexuality – at least, for me. If I'm attracted to women, but don't act on my urges for men, does that still count? What's the difference between bisexual and pansexual? Does bisexuality include attraction to non-binary people? Some people are saying, "Fuck the labels, you love who you love!" Which is perhaps the hippy dippy conclusion I'm at right now.

With all this obsession, it's hardly a surprise that I've partnered up with a man who is bisexual. And if Harry is reading this, then darling I know you don't talk about it much, but I hope you know how much I love and appreciate you for being so supportive, and thank you for being so open about your own experiences with me. You are inspiring and amazing. And if Harry's mum is reading this, then haha just joking Carol and actually I'm not even talking about your son, I'm talking about a different Harry.

So, why did I write this book? Why did I want to come out as bicurious when I'm in a long-term relationship with a man and not yet out to my nan? Well, I want to share these stories with you, I want better representation and I want to explore the many different aspects of what it means. So, dear reader, I gave myself a mission. Could I take a snapshot of my life, my social circle, and find anyone who does or at one point felt like me? Would they be willing to tell me their stories? Surprisingly, many people came forward, and many friends reached out to people in their own lives to spread the word. It was an interesting time in my life, and I felt a huge responsibility in interviewing people. It was just like Louis Theroux but instead of making emotionally intelligent observations, I'd sit there getting drunk and making inappropriate asides. Most people wanted to be off the record and were too stilted in their responses for me to turn into a full chapter. Many people backed out of interviews at the last minute. Many people told me stories that just were too sad or serious. I think writing this book is not just about the stories included, but about the stories that we don't tell, and I hope you'll keep this in mind even as we have fun.

I've tried to be as diverse as I can with these people, though they're mainly the zillenial and millennial experience of bisexuality, considering it's a snapshot from my own life. I wonder, dear reader, what you would find if you took your own snapshot?

Some are very queer, some are very straight, some have different ideals to yours and mine. Some people cheat. Try to remember that anything you come across in this book that you don't like is probably not exclusive to the bisexual experience. Straight and gay people lie and cheat too. In fact, I do want to say to any hetero people reading that I know you don't have it easy either, and I certainly wouldn't want to alienate you by framing the narrative that all the straight people have it all figured out in the bedroom, 'cos you very well may not. Porn addiction is on the rise and many straight women struggle with painful, unfulfilling sex without the option to try it on with a woman instead. And the amount of pressure on hetero men to 'perform' rather than be present is really sad.

But at least you never have to explain what being bisexual is to your nan.

It goes without saying that some people's names, locations, ages and some details in each story have been changed to protect identities. But the anecdotes are true. So, I urge you to be kind to yourself and continue (or start) to be a strong ally of our LGBTQ friends. But in the meantime, sit back, relax and let the bisexuals take the microphone. As I'm told, we do love the attention.

CHAPTER 1:
THE ROSE

I knew I liked women before I liked men. But I didn't know it. Does that make sense? When I was a child, I watched a lot of *Sailor Moon*. This was a Japanese anime on Fox Kids TV, and I would spend hours and hours drawing them in their tiny miniskirts. Their superhero costumes were basically their school uniforms but as if they had shrunk and then paired them with thigh high boots. They stopped airing it after a couple of seasons because the next season introduced the characters Sailor Neptune and Sailor Uranus (ehehehe) who were in a lesbian relationship. Though I think they eventually did air that season and the English dub changed the story so that they were just very, very close cousins. Then came *Tenchi Muyo*, an anime about a normal Japanese student guy surrounded by a harem of beautiful women from outer space who all wanted to be his girlfriend. I'm pretty sure there was an episode where they all went to a spa and Cartoon Network had to digitally alter one of the naked alien women into wearing a swimming cossie. Basically, I watched a ton of soft lesbian anime porn before my age reached double digits. Whoops!

I've no idea if I concerned my parents with this fascination or not, my sisters certainly found it embarrassing when I'd run around the school playground reenacting *Sailor Moon* episodes with my pal Mary.

I would sometimes show my dad said drawings of Sailor Moon or even my own character creations, complete with their own revealing space girl outfits. I'd get the very neutral reply of a divorced weekend dad doing his best to be supportive which was, "Ah yes, very good." Did enjoying these shows make me bicurious? Meh, who knows. Whether it was the chicken or the egg, I knew I enjoyed it. And not in the way I'd enjoyed Disney princesses before. I started getting confused, and the other kids picked up on it. They'd sing a song about me:

Down in the jungle where nobody knows,
There's Thomasin and Mary sexing with no clothes.

Mary was my BFF. We were both very weird, and absolutely warranted bullying. She wore knee high socks when it was cool to wear trainer socks, do you know what I mean? And I was far worse with my greasy hair and braces. It was a song a couple of girls used to sing right to our faces. I remember the searing hot embarrassment rising at the back of my neck as I tried to ignore them. I was hurt! I was hurt because it wasn't true!! I didn't fancy Mary and I didn't like sexing girls. Whatever that meant.

At the age of eleven a boy in my year confided in me at lunch time by the sand pit meant for long jump. It was a quiet area because foxes used the sand pit to do their business. I can't quite remember how we got on the subject, but I remember the anguish in his voice when he said to me, looking out across the field of our care-free peers playing football. "I think I'm gay, but I don't want to be." It was the saddest thing, this child who feared his family and friends were never going to accept him, let alone strangers on the street. He knew he liked boys and he KNEW that he knew it.

But I didn't know anything about myself. I was definitely confused, and I definitely found women enticing in some kind of way, certainly more than the goofy boys in my year. I didn't know that bisexuals existed at that age. So, here's what happened: the kids called me a lesbian...I get confused...and I am, by my nature, dear reader, a *people pleaser*. I am my father's daughter! The kids would say, "You're a lezza!" and I said, "Ah yes, very good."

For the longest time I sincerely thought to myself, they're quite possibly right about me, even though I denied it to their faces. I was like, fuck, I'm probably gay; my Irish Catholic nan is going to hate me. Which is fucking hypocritical because I'm half-convinced that she was a closeted lesbian. My memories are fading of her now, but I basically felt like she was Queen Victoria; a strict, Rubenesque matriarch with a funny accent. I didn't really pick up the Irish twang as a kid, though. She was raised in Lancashire, so it was a bit muddled. She did try to give me some advice about school bullies and their horrible songs with her own cover of a simple rhyme.

Sticks and stones may break my bones
But calling will never hurt me.

So, I'm pretty sure she got this wrong. I'm pretty sure it's supposed to say 'but *names* will never hurt me' or even 'name calling will never hurt me' but she stuck to 'calling' to keep it snappy. The trouble was, the awkward wording was so out of context for me that I didn't understand the moral of the rhyme and kept asking her to repeat it, desperate for some advice for dealing with the bullies. 'Calling' in her accent ended up being interpreted to my childish brain as 'Colin' and after her sagely repeating the rhyme to me again and again I sat back, crossed my arms and thought, "Who the fuck is Colin?"

Anyway, I digress. Like that kid by the sand pit, I didn't want to be different. I distanced myself from Mary and I watched anime on my laptop in secret. Not because it was sexual to me, but because it felt goofy and interesting. But as a teenager it's EMBARRASSING to have niche interests. I tried desperately to be normal, one of my biggest life regrets (alongside that time in 2012 when I dyed my hair purple). I got really into Musical Theatre as I hit secondary school, and it helped with my confidence – the fact that that is one of the queerest hobbies you can have went straight over my head. In school I would daydream about the coolest guy in the year asking me out and finally getting the status of 'cool kid'. But at weekends at Drama School, I'd watch my dance teacher's hips obsessively as she taught the routine, wondering if she had a boyfriend.

It wasn't until I was fifteen years old when I was at a birthday party sleepover where *both* boys and girls attended that I had a realisation. This teenager called Martin caught my eye. He was incredibly obnoxious, not very attractive and very obsessed with getting my friend Liv to be his girlfriend. In short, not the greatest catch *but* he was also an incredible singer and had played Gavroche in *Les Misérables* when he was younger so, as a Musical Theatre geek, I was like oh, hell YES this guy is the ONE.

Anyway, it was gone midnight, we were sleeping next to each other on a large sofa. Liv had earlier made it very clear that although she enjoyed the chase, she was not into him. Without a word to me, Martin tiptoed his hand over to me, slipped his hand under my sleeping bag and started stroking my crotch. I distinctly remember wearing my dark blue denim jeans (what kind of maniac goes to sleep in jeans?!) and there being a safe barrier between my skin and his light touch. But despite this, I remember feeling something incredibly new in my nether regions, electricity, a tingle, a pulsation that fell to the whim of his wandering hand. Basically, all the cliche things you hear when someone is fucking turned on. And I just remember my first thought was, "Oh thank god – I'm not a lesbian."

So that was that. No horrible conversations to my nan about coming out. I was straight after all! I had just been a bit confused but now I was maturing into an adult and all the adult things with it, including sex. I went on to spend the next decade dating men with a few drunken snogs with female friends thrown in to truly cement the straight girl experience. The latter never felt like I was giving in to any sexual urges though; it felt daring at best but sadly, more performative for my boyfriends and the thrill of doing something taboo (sometimes we bring these problems on ourselves). I was a basic bitch. A nice and well-meaning bitch, of course, but basic. To be honest, it's been tough trying to explain these desires to male partners. I often felt like my bisexuality was bastardised by ex-partners that I was open about it with, being used for their own sexual gratification rather than a shared experience. This only got worse as I grew older and still remained firmly inexperienced with women. The idea of a threesome was fun but why should I share anything with anyone when I haven't even had anything on my own merit? I was frozen, caught between genuinely wanting to turn on my boyfriend and feeling resentful. There was one ex, where during dirty talk he wouldn't stop talking about girls he'd like to see me with. I distinctly remember thinking, "Get. Your hands. OFF. My bicuriousity." Which is not a good thought, really. He wasn't a mind reader, and I was so fucking agreeable in the relationship that I didn't make it clear as to why I was uncomfortable – and due to the visible discomfort, I think he ended up thinking I was all talk, that I was indeed 'performative.' A fraud. And I felt that too.

What further added to my confusion about my sexuality was the fact that none of my boyfriends were making me orgasm. I'm cringing as I write this, it's honestly embarrassing to admit and I really hope I don't regret being so open, but it's part of my story and I do think we need to talk about it more. Forget the gender pay gap, I want to talk about the gender cum gap. I *know* I am not the only woman who has been attracted to men but still struggled to enjoy fulfilling sex or finding the confidence to explore what they want. So, if by any chance you're a bisexual or bicurious person reading this and is also having trouble with getting what you need sexually (god maybe this is a niche demographic I'm going for), I also want to declare that THERE IS NOTHING WRONG WITH YOU (AGAIN). It wasn't until I was in my mid-twenties and I met an Italian nurse that it happened for me. I think my attraction to his Sicilian olive skin and dark eyes combined with his knowledge of female anatomy did the job. Going forward, I've had no problems and I'm having a lot of fun with my current boyfriend making up for lost time. That last part isn't integral to the story by the way; I just want to show off and advertise my sequel book: *Why Straight Women Come Last: Accounts of bad sex and happy endings.* (Look at me, only on chapter one of my first book and already trying to plug my second. What a capitalist.)

The fact that I wasn't being fulfilled sexually again brought up fears that maybe I had gotten it wrong after all. Maybe Martin was a fluke. Maybe being attracted to men was just a trick I'd played on myself to try and be normal. Because of this, I've always felt like I should be a lot gayer than I actually turned out to be. Maybe a lot of women are bicurious for the same reason. There are straight women who watch lesbian porn. Maybe if that's titillating them but meanwhile their boyfriend isn't able to help them out, they're sat there wondering whether they're gay. Maybe some of them are. But I have a feeling it's more complex than that. Sexuality *is* complex, gay or straight.

It's not that I was having a bad time – sex felt really good, but nothing seemed to dig deep enough (not literally, I have to say, darlings). Was I being stimulated by the wrong sex? An ex-boyfriend of mine certainly delighted in my theory so his own perceived shortcomings could be let off the hook. He loudly proclaimed in the street as he walked me one time to our first – and only – couples counselling session, "Yes, that's what's leading to all of our problems, maybe you're GAAAAY. Maybe you're a LESBIAN." He said it so loudly that people in the street heard, and a familiar hot flush of embarrassment from my childhood seared through me once again, and I felt terribly ashamed. Not at the thought of being gay, but for not really knowing whether he was right.

I tried lesbian speed dating with a gay friend of mine, Louise. I thought it would be a fun way to meet lots of women really quickly and figure out my type. We were both rubbish at it. Louise chose the only emotionally unavailable woman in the room, and I had no idea how to flirt with women, so I just asked them all about their hair care regimes. I left with some sound advice but zero fanny.

I would also second guess myself when I had interactions with women that I didn't find attractive. Obviously, even though I'm attracted to men, I'm not going to desire every single man that flirts with me. Somehow, I had forgotten this vital piece of common sense when it came to women. If I didn't like a woman, I took it as evidence of my heterosexuality. One time, when I half crashed, half volunteered to get up on stage at a Drag Queen Cabaret night, after declaring my bicuriousity to the crowd (it was relevant to the conversation I promiiiise), I had a woman come up to me afterwards. She was pretty, but a complete stranger. She flirted with me loudly over the music as I stood there like a mannequin. She started touching my hips. We danced closely together. Well, I say, 'we'…she was very energetic and kind of bumped up against me. It was a bit like when you hit a helium balloon and it bobs around a little by itself. It looks like the balloon is vibing, but really, it's a cry for help. I looked over to my friends for aid and they all gave me a thumbs up with huge grins. *Get in there!* Ah, shit, no help there. I, ever the people-pleaser, continued to bob.

Alright, so, at this stage you might be thinking, 'Thomasin, you're right. You're really not as gay as you think you are.' Which is what I thought too. I even declared it to this guy I was seeing before Italian Nurse. This guy (We'll call him Mr Bojangles) was also definitely attractive to me and still failed to make me climax during sex. He never tried to explore my attraction to women or impart his own opinion on the subject, which I really appreciated. In hindsight, I think that was down to his general disconnect with our relationship than being respectful. And he didn't have much sympathy or insight as to why he was failing to get me off. "Well I've made plenty of girls cum before soooo…" *It's a 'you' problem.* That was the message I got. I mean it *was* a me problem, but after eight minutes with Italian Nurse I wanted to line up all my previous partners and yell at them. You couldn't spare EIGHT minutes on undivided, vanilla attention? Really? I'd never thought to ask for that time myself because I was in this vicious cycle of 'it just doesn't happen for me.' And as a people-pleaser, I was all about giving them what they wanted. I didn't want to feel seen. My people-pleasing did start to wear off with Bojangles though. At this stage I was twenty-five with a fully developed frontal lobe, a failed career in Musical Theatre and a better understanding that there is no such thing as normal, actually. Once I yelled in his face right in the heat of us getting it on, super horny and super unfulfilled, "I'M. SO. FRUSTRATED." Whoops. We both politely ignored that. So, I was ready to admit to myself that my bicuriousity had bloomed in the mess of all this, only to realise, "Ohhhh, I'm not bi. I'm just having bad sex."

And then I saw her.

Well, technically him. It was a Drag King and the 'she' playing a 'he' was absolutely stunning to me. And not in the way that hetero girls call other hetero girls stunning.

Mr Bojangles had taken me on a date to see a drag-themed improvised musical and this girl, we'll call Lisa, was playing one of the parts. I'd never seen a Drag King before and I was mesmerised by all of them, frankly. These women looked so incredibly masculine but maintained a camp air of grace with their pencil thin moustaches and dainty wrists.

AND THEY COULD ALL SING AND IMPROVISE
SHOW-STOPPING MUSICAL THEATRE BALLADS!!
Just like how I was enthralled with Martin, I found myself
wanting Lisa.

yoo
hoo

I maybe would have forgotten about her, but it turned
out by some sort of destiny that Lisa and I had mutual
friends. We somehow ended up on a mutual WhatsApp
group for a creative Londoners group (basically a meet-up to
stop people from procrastinating, but really all people do is

plug their own work). There were about thirty people on it, and strictly business. I got to see her dressed down and she was every bit as stunning as I imagined her to be. Long brown hair, an angelic face and heaps and heaps of talent. I learned through friends that Lisa was an accomplished creative in many ways, not just through improvising musicals. I thought she was so fucking cool and so beautiful, and I found myself wondering what I'd do if I was single. I mean, I already had her number, basically! But I kept my thoughts completely to myself.

Time went on, My Bojangles and I ended. I then dated Italian Nurse for six months and although it was my shortest long-term relationship, I am still to this day grateful for what he did for me. I think these experiences made me realise how I was definitely still attracted to men. They made me feel things. Italian Nurse gave me pleasure, Bojangles gave me pain. A lot of pain.

In short, it turns out I was some sort of side piece to a long-distance relationship he was having. We broke up and not even a month later – when friends verified he was still *very much* with his long distance girlfriend – I saw him pulling the same shit, bringing another girl at a party he was very aware I was going to, openly making out with her. He ignored me the whole time, probably terrified I'd reveal the truth to his new side piece. You know what sucks, dear reader? I had a feeling the whole time it would end this way. I could feel him pulling away as I pulled closer. I could feel him picking fights and making thinly veiled criticisms of me. I was willing to go through a whole lot of heartache for just a little bit of cock. And not even a particularly talented cock. It was a triple threat cock, you know? It couldn't dance, it couldn't sing, and it couldn't make me cum. He wasn't even a very clever or kind man. But he was a man. And I was willing to be a loser to keep it. *That* was how straight I was. And then once I had my relationship with Italian nurse where I had of course experienced a sexual pleasure that I hadn't previously, I knew for sure how I felt. I knew I liked men and I KNEW it. Hallelujah! But the thoughts of many women still lingered in my mind. I was still curious.

Italian Nurse and I parted on good terms, it was simply a split on different lifetime wants (he wanted to live in a van and I didn't). Valentine's Day was coming around. Another Drag Improv Musical was showing on February 14th, and I'd made up my mind; I was going to watch the show and I was going to say hi to Lisa. Fuck it! Life isn't a dress rehearsal, this is the show! Let's do it.

I invited some friends from an improv class I'd been taking to go see this show and make it a fun night out – so even if things went wrong with Lisa, I could still hang out with my buddies. I worked a full shift at the cake shop Cutter & Squidge on Valentine's Day. My manager was super sweet and bought a load of single red roses to give out to each of the staff members. He gave mine to me and it had a tag on it:

Dear Thomasin
Happy Valentine's Day!
From
The Management Team at Cutter & Squidge

Not the most personal of sign-offs but still it was a lovely gesture. I gave him a hug and thanked him, placing it in my tote bag. The shift ended, I put on my make-up and got ready to leave for the Drag show. As I was leaving, by the door I noticed some single, untagged red roses in a bucket of water. Inspiration struck.

"Hey can I take one of these roses?"

"Sure! They'll be binned otherwise; they were leftovers."

I placed another in my tote bag. How romantic I was going to be to Lisa! I pictured what I was going to say, walking up to her after the show ended and handing her a single red rose. "That was an amazing show! I just wanted to give you this rose seeing as it's Valentine's Day, just to say how much I loved it! You don't know me but I'm Thomasin, I'm friends with Josh and Richard. We're actually on a WhatsApp group together!" And then we'd talk a bit and I'd leave, maybe using that as a cue to drop her a text later depending on how it went. It was important to note about us being on the same WhatsApp group so she wouldn't freak out that I'd gotten her number from nowhere. It was a very big move, in hindsight. But I wasn't used to wooing women! It took me a long enough time to woo men, to be honest. The first date I ever went on with a guy in sixth form was a disaster. We went for a walk in the park (because we were teenagers and had no money). It was going well; the sun was shining, we were laughing. We'd been walking apart from each other when suddenly he touched the small of my back and this charge of electricity went through my body – and much like Martin – I didn't know what to do with the intense feeling or how I should respond so I yelled, "BUSH PUSH!" and then I pushed him into a bush. I now know in my infinite wisdom after dating men for several years that that's not what you should do. With Lisa, it was like I was a teenager again; I felt clueless as if the difference in gender had cut through all of my life experience at this point.

But off I went! We watched the show and it was – just like the last time – brilliant. Lisa shone in the cast, quite literally in a sequined blazer and glittered sideburns. They even took my friend Luka's suggestion for a setting for the improv, "A DUNGEON!" I love my friends.

We had a wonderful evening. It was the first Valentine's Day that I'd been single for a long while and it was refreshing to celebrate it as a single woman. The moment of truth came. To leave the venue, the audience had to walk across the stage to the exit. The cast were standing by the door, thanking everyone for coming as they left. I could see Lisa chatting and laughing to some audience members. My heart started pounding in my chest. I got cold sweats. My moment of truth came. I met her face-to-face and opened my mouth to speak. And guess what, dear reader? I married her. No just kidding, it was a disaster.

So, it was off to a weird start. First of all, I was standing way too close to her even by the standards of the pre-pandemic times. And also, because I was nervous, I spoke way too quickly. I could see the glitter that had dropped off her eyebrows and onto her eyelashes and under her eyes. She was beautiful and, in an effort to not be nervous and show emotion, I turned into a malfunctioning robot.

"THATWASREALLYAMAZINGTHANKYOUYOU' RESOBRILLIANT, AND I justwantedtogive YOUTHIS."

Without even looking at the rose I pulled it out of my bag with all the care and speed of pulling a broken umbrella out when it starts raining. I thrust it into her hands. "JUSTcos you're working on VALENTINE'SDAY and I JUSTWANTED TOSAYYOUWERE AMAZING. We actually know each other. On WhatsApp. We're on a group together. You knOWJOSHANDRICHARD. Soyeah." *Nailed it.*

I was so anxious! I wasn't just flirting with a woman I liked, it was flirting with the FIRST woman I liked. And she looked kind of scared of this weird robot standing way too close to her. She clutched the rose with a frozen smile. "Oh my gosh. Thank you…so much!" At the time I took it as her being shy, but in hindsight it was most likely awkwardness. From my memory, the rest of the drag cast watched in silence. Had the world stopped?

I bid her farewell, "Cool. Well, have a good night. Well done again!" And I skipped off to celebrate with my friends. Because at the time, dear reader, I thought that had gone very well. I honestly really did. I was deluded. I'd always thought I had a good grasp on recognising when a guy liked me, and although I can be bashful, I also know how to flirt, and any awkwardness I've been able to play off as quirky and charming (at least that's what I've been telling myself this whole time). "Look at me in my dungarees and short hair, I don't know how to flirt ha ha *haaaa*. Let's go out some time though."

I'd done the right thing, right?! I didn't want a repeat of the speed dating when I ended up speaking too platonically so I'd just gone for it – red rose and everything. I was very sad to realise, upon reflection, that if I'd been a guy then I would have come across as a complete creep! Oh noooo! :(My first bisexual experiment and I'm CREEPY. Suddenly I felt myself having a new sense of empathy for the characters on *The Inbetweeners*.

But anyway, *at the time* I thought I had been super romantic and cute to this complete stranger. I went and got drunk with my friends at the bar, celebrating a successful life as a bisexual lady and a joyous Valentine's Day.

The night ended. My friends and I parted ways. I sat down at Waterloo underground station, waiting for the Northern line to take me home. I was exhausted! I set my tote bag on the floor, not caring for the ratty germs on the

27

ground of the tube platform. I saw my rose from work peeking out and picked it up to play with. I pulled it out and noticed the tag had come off. That was weird! I started looking in my tote bag for the tag. Not there. Huh. Wait.

Oh. Oh no. OH NO.

I'd given Lisa the wrong rose. And just in case you forgot what it said, it was:

Dear Thomasin
Happy Valentine's Day!
From
The Management Team at Cutter & Squidge

So not only had I been way too forward with Lisa with an overly romantic gesture, I'd also made it look like I'd *regifted my creepy rose.*

Panicking, I opened WhatsApp and found her number from our mutual group. I drunkenly typed in:

So I think I gave you the rose that work made me! Cos they made me 2 and mine was tagged! Unless it fell off?

And then after no reply, another:

Well done again for tonight, my friends and I absolutely loved it.

I'm starting to think God has kept me away from women for good reason.

She, of course, did not text back.

Turns out she had a girlfriend anyway. What can ya do, am I right fellas?!

It was an embarrassing failure, but I knew at least where I stood internally now. Just like my idiocy with going after Mr Bojangles, I discovered that I *definitely* liked women enough to be willing to make an arse of myself. So, it was an important lesson for me (or at least that's what I tell myself when a cringe attack comes on at 1 am as the memory infiltrates my unguarded brain). And if I could apologise to her for making her feel awkward, I would. But the best thing to do is just to never go to any drag improv musical shows ever again.

So, I'm afraid my story ends here, dear reader. Literally one week later, I met my current partner, Harry. I played it somewhat more cool with him and didn't unleash the crazy until about a month in. We're still going strong as of me typing this. I always worried with previous boyfriends that I was missing some sort of experience or aspect of my sexuality, but I really don't feel that way at all now. I may be bicurious, but I'm no longer curious. The conclusion, dear reader, is that I'd love to claim the post of bisexual, but for one reason or another, I've just not clocked in the hours. I don't feel comfortable with that as a label for myself when so much of my experience has been juvenile. Maybe it's something I'll explore at a later stage, but haven't I done enough overthinking to last me a lifetime? How about we move on? It's time to meet some other sluts and frauds.

CHAPTER 2:
SPEAKING FRENCH

If you were to ask me to show you a picture of a bisexual man, it would probably be of an Elf King from the film adaptations of *Lord of the Rings*. Think of Legolas or Arwen's dad – you know, the one played by Hugo Weaving? Or Galadriel's husband.

They're all fabulous gowns, shiny hair and chiselled jaws. I don't know why but I get major bi vibes from the lot of them. Also David Bowie, but that's kind of obvious. Why am I telling you this? Because that's pretty much what Florian looks like.

Florian Hencher is quite possibly the most enchanting man I've ever known. Granted, I'm biased; he is a very good friend of mine. He moves like a dancer but is forthright like a warrior, lifting his teacup with the poise of a queen then slams it down excitedly when a new thought comes. He's a writer, actor, photographer, director and all-round creative genius. His passion is fantasy photoshoots, and he's often dressed as an elf or Viking or prince (or sometimes all three) and pictured in forest surroundings (it's plastered all over his social media, but I rather think he does it even when no one is watching).

We're on holiday in Edinburgh, a wonderful place for writing inspiration. We tuck ourselves into the very back corner of Kilimanjaro, a cute little cafe in the city centre that thankfully doesn't claim to be where JK Rowling wrote *Harry Potter* just because she once came in for a croissant. Florian comes to my interview casually dressed in jeans and a flannel shirt, his shining blonde hair bouncing off his face. Florian's very aware of his androgynous facial features. "From the side on I've got quite a masculine profile, I've got quite a strong jaw, but face-on I've got quite feminine features. There's something for everyone!"

Florian is incredibly at ease in his skin. He's been in a long-term relationship with a man for many years, and despite often being mistaken as gay, he's confident that he's bisexual, and it's not something he's supposedly 'lost' for choosing to be with a man. Speaking of losing, "I lost my virginity at fifteen to a girl and started fooling around with boys at that age too. I felt that *both* were attracted to me." Florian shrugs. "Maybe that's why I've always been comfortable with who I am." No overthinking for this one.

I'm curious to know how he's navigated things but for Florian, there was never a moment where he came out as bisexual to his family or friends.

"I've not got a coming out story. I've dated both men and women. Every time an encounter or relationship ended with a man, I found myself going back to women – not as a way to eradicate that, but if I met a woman through my work or something." He admits to me, "You know it was definitely *easier* dating women from the perspective of how people view you – like introducing them to families. Whereas with a man it took a lot longer for me to feel comfortable enough to introduce him because you feel like you have to give an explanation. You know, reminding them that no it wasn't a phase and it's still a possibility. And no, I'm not gay now. I'm who I've always been."

Despite this, Florian found exploring his sexuality with his own gender would move a lot quicker – in private, at least. "Growing up at school with the other boys, I never made the first move. I'd have school friends in my room, the conversation came up like 'have you ever done this before, have you ever kissed a guy before' etcetera and then before you know it you're experimenting."

Florian recalls a time in French class – a subject that he enjoyed and excelled at, and a language he still speaks today. He's there concentrating on his past and future tense sentences. Suddenly a boy in his class turns around to look at him. What does he want? "We'll call him John," Florian says with a grin. "He was a very popular guy, like a footballer. He leant over to me and said, 'I want you to touch my dick.' And my first thought was 'oh my god how disrespectful' and my second thought was 'can you say that in French please?'"

John continues to push. "He goes on like, 'have you ever thought about that?' We're literally at the back of French class having this conversation."

Florian's not one to be appalled easily, but in his retelling of the memory, he sounds annoyed, almost disgusted with John. I think the story's going in another direction but then he promptly says, "Anyway then we walked home together, went into a big cornfield and we experimented. My school bag landed in a muddy puddle and when I pulled out my textbooks to do homework later that night, my French book was all soggy. Worth it."

I'm slightly taken aback by the forward nature of this at such a young age. Girl to girl there's always seemed to be a bit of pussyfooting around the subject (maybe that's where they get that word from).

Florian believes it's natural to experiment with your own gender as a teenager, even for straight people. "I think this happens a lot more than we talk about." I ask him if it ever felt awkward. I mean, what do you talk about after?

"I felt like how I'd imagine an adult feels after a one-night stand. You'd go back to school and pretend as if nothing had happened. You'd never address it. It was just an experience."

Florian's aware of how wild it all sounds, but "running through fields of wheat" as he puts it was common for all the teenagers then. "I lived in a village near the countryside in Cornwall. As an adult I sometimes wish my life was still that exciting. When you're young you don't talk about things, you're not really sure what you're doing at that stage even though you're physically almost a fully developed man. And it's been that way throughout history. Think of England in the 1500s and how repressed *they* were. But it's like your impulses are so strong you're not thinking straight!" Literally or figuratively. It wasn't always idyllic, and Florian shakes his head as he suddenly recalls the shame. It hits him and he drops the air of nonchalance for a moment. "After that experience with John I did feel dirty. Like, did I want to do that? I almost didn't recognise myself."

I ask what happened next. Florian looks down at his tea-cup. "I never discussed it with John again. French class was never the same. Of all the classes for it to happen in as well!" He sighs wistfully, looking off into the distance, "It's the Parisian way." Speaking of Paris, Florian would later go on to have his first relationship with a man at Disneyland Paris. With no less than Prince Charming himself. A half-French, half-American man named Tristan. But back at school, Florian's first intense crush was on a girl called Amy. At the age of fifteen, she's in his school year and the most gorgeous girl in the school. He remarks on her long, red hair and I smile to myself. Even as his friend now, I know he still has a thing for girls with long red hair. I guess Amy was the original. Florian, being the most gorgeous boy in the school, naturally was paired with Amy and they dated for a while. It turns out long red hair can't hide an unimaginative personality, and it soon fizzled out in an uncharacteristically undramatic way for a first teenage romance. From there he dated another girl called Hannah. Florian doesn't say much about Hannah except that she broke his heart. He calls this his "official" relationship as a way of explaining that they were sexually active. Florian enjoyed himself.

"When I first was with a girl there was not a part of me wishing I was with a man – but I knew deep inside me that I had that desire." Much to his surprise, he found himself more open about his bisexuality in the couple of hours spent with John, when all the cards were on the table (and all trousers on the ground), than the long months with his girlfriend. Months are very long when you're a teenager, if you recall.

"I've experienced both of my repression actually from women more so than men. Men make fun of things that are a bit girly mostly because they feel that it's socially what they should do. But getting close to girls, if they detected that there was anything feminine about me then they were insecure about that. I did ballet from the age of seven and I'm

36

very lucky that my parents were willing to let me explore myself in that way, but I felt like the girls made me very aware that I was the only boy in the class.

"My family are all very young looking. I didn't really blossom into my manhood until I was in my twenties. At fifteen my face was developing, and I didn't look like a child by any stretch, but my body was still so young compared to everyone else, especially the girls! I had the face of a grown man on this slim body. This girl in dance class said to me, 'how come your body is skinny but your jawline is defined.'" He grumbles at our now empty plates, wiping cake crumbs off his hands and says, "Funnily enough as an adult I'm trying to get back to that skinny shape."

"Don't be ridiculous," I scoff. Dear reader, this man is a professional model.

Florian continues. "But that shaming culture comes a lot from women. Women are allowed to have a preference to what they want their men to be like, they're kind of allowed to be mean about looks in a way I couldn't get away with. But when they're projecting that onto every man, not just love interests, just because they don't meet their expectations, I mean Thomasin you really feel that shame. Just like how men do it to women. It's bad there too, of course. I've seen men tell women that they'd look better with long hair and it's wrong – go find that person then! Don't make someone feel ashamed that they don't meet their expectations! Our image is for us." The judgement from women is what put Florian off exploring his bisexuality any further for a while. The wheat fields remained empty, his French textbooks dry and Florian did pirouettes in his dance class, trying to ignore the girls giggling. Florian admits, "I'd never had a man make me feel that way."

Florian had aspirations of being an actor. When he turned nineteen his elfin face was cast perfectly as Peter Pan at Disneyland Paris. He broke up with the girl he'd been dating after Hannah the Heartbreaker. Her name was Rosie. He smirks. "Rosie was a good Christian girl, there were a lot of occasions where we didn't have sex only because she wanted to wait for marriage. But we still did other things. She was a beautiful model. I got the job to Disneyland Paris and she broke up with me as she met the son of a pastor and went on fulfil her dream of being a good Christian wife and having sex." Win-win, feeling good.

Enter Tristan.

Tristan was a gay French-American and cast as Prince Charming at Disneyland, and when he walked into the room Florian was besotted.

"With Tristan it was love at first sight. In fact, all of the people I've been in relationships with had an intensely love-at-first-sight experience. It was the first time I was swept off my feet. He played the character Prince Charming at Disneyland Paris for both me and the public. I didn't go to Disneyland to meet Cinderella, *I* was Cinderella!" Away from home for the first time, Florian's relationship with Tristan was able to flourish, slipping in easily amongst the other performers of Disneyland. A good size of the cast identified as LGBTQ.

I imagine that it may have been nerve wracking to be fully intimate with a man for the first time, but Florian felt very safe with Tristan. "The experience made me fall in love with him, and fall in love with bisexuality. I'd already known I was attracted to men and had dealt with that but this was the first time that I could embrace it and act on it. I remember him putting his arm around me, this bigger form comforting me. That's where the love happened. It's like, 'wow we're married now!'" Florian sits back, almost euphoric at the memory. "Everybody deserves that feeling," he adds. And then they were at it like rabbits.

Just like how I felt like I was regressing with my teenage-like crush on Lisa the Drag King, Florian felt all the intense, dramatic feelings he'd had with Hannah The Heartbreaker. "It was painful to not be with him, I'd forgotten what it was like when I was fifteen and in love. But with Hannah I was *allowed* Hannah, that was purely just young love figuring itself out. But with Tristan it was like a release of an oppression that I didn't know I'd even had." This would go on to be the basis of their first argument, four months into the relationship. One evening, as they're making dinner together after another passionate round of sex, Tristan is encouraging Florian to admit he's gay. Florian, although young, is sure of himself and won't budge. But he does admit the new, intense thrill of giving in to his love for men.

"Tristan couldn't get it, he said, 'did you not feel a kind of release?' And he thought I was coming out, but I had to make it clear that this was not me coming out, I knew I still liked women. He thought I was in denial. He just couldn't relate to that. Sex with women for him was oppressive and forced whereas although I genuinely did feel a release, I didn't want that love for women to be undermined. Because it wasn't me coming out. Being gay wasn't a choice for Tristan. For me, choosing to be in a relationship with him, it was a choice but it *wasn't* a choice. Do you know what I mean?"

Tristan and Florian would split up over long distance issues once their contracts ended.

After Tristan, Florian dated an American beauty queen called Nicole for three years. Because of course he did.

"When Tristan found out I was dating a woman he said, 'So who is this BEETCH you're fucking now.' He wrote her off completely because she was a woman. Until he did that later when I was dating another guy, 'Who is this DEECK you're dating.' And I was like, ohhhh, he's not sexist, he's just jealous."

I wonder if there is a part of Florian, when dating a woman after a man, that feels, *I forgot how to do this!* Florian doesn't try to pretend. "Yes. Every time. But you just get through it because you get sexually attracted to that person.

I still have days that I crave the opposite sex. But it's no different to say, say if you're with a man with a particular shaped dick and you miss another type of dick and you just miss that. It's the same thing, you just have to deal with the fact that you've chosen this other dick."

Florian and Nicole were incredibly in love. Florian talks of her like she was a goddess. He ponders as to why such a hyper feminine woman would choose someone with his own feminine, androgynous looks, perhaps because his gentler approach and outwardly softer appearance was safer. "The kind of men I'd see hit on Nicole were the conventional tall, muscular men. Beautiful, hyper-masculine men. They'd hit on her almost aggressively and she was very intimidated by that. I actually saw her really recoil. She was never going to be with someone like that, you know." Though they were certainly Florian's type. "It was like, she's not interested, but I'll take that! 'Get away from her! Buuut you're fine with me.'"

"She was intellectually attracted to me. She made me feel attractive physically too, and I think there was a comfortability in the fact that we were both empowered in the feminine." I picture Galadriel and Legolas side by side at the bar, turning down the hobbits.

Determined not to go through the same long-distance issues as he'd had with Tristan, Florian moved out to the US to be with Nicole. They discussed marriage with the plan that Nicole would return to the UK with him on an engagement visa. It seemed like he'd found 'it'. But they were both young and too focused on their own goals. Nicole wasn't ready to uproot her life. Florian returned to the UK alone and heartbroken. At just twenty-four years old, he'd broken up with two great lovers over long-distance. He wasn't looking for another serious relationship for a while.

Enter Heather.

Heather was his work colleague at a yoga health shop, and he was unable to hide his attraction to her. Another love-at-first sight, they immediately joked over yoga mats and green tea. It was freeing to flirt again. Namaste.

"With Heather, it was a rebound at the beginning. It wasn't long after Nicole and she was still in my thoughts." Florian's relationship with Heather was volatile. "Sex with Heather was one of the first times I'd been with a girl who was more experienced than I was. She was older than me and she had a sexual appetite. I was learning a lot of positions that I didn't know girls liked! It was a lot of sex, sex, sex."

Florian thought they were on the same page, just work colleagues with benefits (because *that's such a good idea*!!!). "I thought we were having fun but then she wanted commitment. We broke up a few times in the eighteen months we were together. She was ready for things that I wasn't. We also had a pregnancy scare, which didn't help. I was scared – *really* scared – about that. I guess I got the whole hetero experience with Heather. How immersive."

To take the pressure off their relationship, Florian found a new job at a bookshop.

"It's funny. With Heather, I chased her. With Nicole, I chased her. Then here we go again; I was being pursued by a guy. And his voice made me melt. It was so posh! 'Hoi Oim Jay.' And wow, such presence in the room."

Florian describes Jay's blonde hair and brown eyes ("Picture a younger, gender swapped Britney Spears"). They meet on Florian's first day. Florian reaches out his hand to shake Jay's.

Immediate electricity. Oh no.

It was clearly the start of something exciting. If it was a movie, this is where the violin strings would come soaring in.

"And all I could think was, wow, hate him. HATE HIM."

The violins scratch to a halt. "What?!" I say.

"Yep. Straight up hated him. I was rejecting him because I was with someone. It was like I'm *going* to hate this person because I need to reject this powerful interaction."

I thought of my own interactions. I tell Florian about the first date I went on and how I pushed the guy into the bushes because I couldn't handle the physical attraction. Florian is both flummoxed and entertained by teenage Thomasin's lack of grace. I was not pulling anyone into any fields any time soon.

"'BUSH PUSH!'" As he quotes me, he is wiping away tears with his napkin.

"I know, I know," I say.

"You can't just do that."

"*I know.*"

"You can't just add a cute rhyme to a crime and call it flirting."

"I KNOW. Honestly, I might as well have brandished a knife, yelled 'knifey poke' and stabbed him up while saying, 'I'm not like other girls.'"

I can't imagine Florian hasn't ever had a human moment like this. "Come on, you must have done something stupid around Jay."

Florian sniffs and replies, "No, not me. Jay did though. Jay threw a stapler at my head."

Ouch.

"And I thought, that is the man for me. Oh god!"

The stapler hits Florian in the back of the head as he's restocking a shelf. He's as cool as a cucumber, turns around and narrows his eyes in venom at Jay, resisting the urge to start rubbing his sore head. Florian has the kind of coloured eyes that turn different shades under different lighting. Sometimes they're blue, sometimes they're green, but when he narrows them in anger, you could swear they almost turn black.

He says eerily calmly to Jay, "What did you do that for?"

Jay goes silent, frozen in fear or excitement. "I dunno."

Personally, I'm disappointed in Jay. He didn't even have a pun ready like, "Just thought that you should...*pull yourself together.*" (No, I'm sorry for that pun please keep reading, please ignore me).

44

The worst part was that Florian thought Jay was straight. "I thought it was a straight guy trying to be assertive. Just lobbing this stapler at me like"—he mimes a rugby throw—"'NYEH!' I thought he was alpha presenting when now I recognise it as violently awkward flirting!" Florian's way of dealing with it was ignoring him but then constantly looking for him around the shop.

"I put myself in his presence purely to reject him. I'd be like 'Where is he? Is he looking at me? Is he looking?!' And a colleague would be like, 'Yeah he is.' And I'd be like, 'Ugh!'" He mimes storming off and then not so slyly looking over his shoulder to see if he was being chased. It's cartoonish, and not subtle. Everyone had caught on to the cat and mouse they were playing.

"Once Heather came in to work to see me and I caught him looking at us. I thought, 'Is he looking at her!?' I just grabbed her hand and walked her upstairs to the staff room. I was asserting that she was *mine*.

"Later on, we finished a shift together, closing up the shop. I was polite, 'Do you need a lift?' Jay lied about which way he was going in order to get taken in my car. He had to confess when I was driving. I was like, 'So where are we going?' And he says quietly, 'It's the other way.' It was so awkward," he says affectionately.

They converse properly for the first time on that car journey. "Jay was intelligent. He was always one step ahead of me. I casually said, 'So are you with someone?' and he immediately says, 'Do you mean am I with a man?' He knew what the conversation was. I found out he was also bisexual. I dropped him off and said, not really thinking about it, 'We should go to the cinema sometime.'"

Jay replies, "Okay. It's date."

Enter Jay.

"No, no, no!" Florian says. "I started panicking, I'm like, wait, I'm with Heather!"

Both actors, Jay and Florian both had a flair for the dramatic. They proceeded to act out different films in their heads. For Jay, he and Florian were twirling around each other, pursuing a love/hate work romance in a cute romcom. For Florian, he was going through a heavy relationship drama, trying to keep Heather happy. Jay is in *Fifty First Dates* and Florian is in *Marriage Story*. "Jay didn't know why I was ignoring him, he tried to get me alone in the stock room, he tried to initiate things, but I just swooped under his arm saying, 'Not here!' It was all very melodramatic." Heather appeared to have spider senses, showing up to work unannounced a couple of times. Florian believes she may have suspected he was seeing a girl from work. He'd go from one moment escaping Jay from the stock room to hearing that Heather had arrived unexpectedly and jumping straight back into the stock room to hide. Florian tried to hold out. He explains, "Sometimes you're in a relationship and you get attracted to another person and it's fine, you just don't act on it."

But the writing was on the wall. Florian ended things with Heather and two weeks later he went on a first date with Jay. After months of sexual tension, Florian once again felt a powerful release. "We planned to make a Sunday roast but we never got to the roast. I remember just lying there with him after it all, covered in..." He trails off. Gravy?

"I'm actually writing an erotic novel about the realities of gay sex, it's all very unrealistic in the rare times that it's portrayed. I think it's great when you're covered in your own...*love making*. It's great!" Jay and Florian went on to date for two and a half years. Not one more stapler was thrown.

I must confess, dear reader. This book is meant to be about embarrassing accounts, but Florian is by all definitions of the word, a 'successful' bisexual. He's moved between different lovers with ease and established both good sex and meaningful relationships. In terms of Florian's journey towards self-acceptance, I find it's actually in his childhood. Even then, he's incredibly self-aware.

"As a child you discover a lot of your sexuality through child's play. From the age of five I played with boys toys, action men and cars. Then when my younger cousin grew older, she played with Barbie dolls, and I remember the first time I saw the *Little Mermaid* doll...it was the first time I was attracted to playing with a girl's toy. I think that's when my family started to recognise it."

He describes the *Little Mermaid* toy, "It was the hair. The aesthetic of red hair and the mermaid tail." I think of young Amy and her long, red hair. I think of Nicole the Beauty Queen. I smile and Florian nods. He adds, "It's strange that toys can start to give away a child's future sexuality."

"I had a very camp grandmother, and she clearly wanted a granddaughter. I was her first grandchild. I think she enjoyed expressing herself – and I didn't reject that. My grandfather's exact words were 'Don't let him play with dolls you'll turn him queer.'"

Did Florian understand what that meant, at such a young age?

"No but I knew it had something to do with being girlish, I knew that being girlish was wrong, so I understood from an early age to be ashamed of anything feminine and female.

"My grandmother was a bit of a drunk. After 6 pm she tried her best to – not beat it – but you know, she used to be too honest. Stuff like, 'We should not let you play with this, I'm worried about you for when you grow up.' It was very confusing as a child. I think she herself was scared of what it was doing to me as a child and how I'd be like in school and how it would affect my childhood.

"They would try to take the dolls away but then when she was sober, she'd put them back in my hand! It was very 'Here you go – NO.' That was my first encounter with the conflict of male and female. I was very much not allowed to be fluid. My first encounter with understanding that I was attracted to the male form was, I was maybe ten years old. I remember *Johnny Bravo* being on the TV and I remember just this hunky, muscular, body. I had a very different reaction to it."

If you don't know, Johnny Bravo was the titular character on the Cartoon Network show, with sunglasses and a box of a chest with a square jaw and short, little legs. Johnny Bravo definitely skipped leg day. But the character is hyper-masculine and flirty. Good looking but also chaotic and rarely successful. I think he's partially modelled on Elvis Presley.

"And I remember thinking why am I attracted to this? And not really understanding why…and I remember being physically attracted to a certain shape in a man which is, I've dated that!" I think of Tristan the Prince Charming and Jay the stapler-throwing bookshop clerk. Florian ponders the chicken-or-the-egg question. "It's strange that the women have replicated *The Little Mermaid* and the men have replicated *Johnny Bravo*." So, few of us are able to make childhood dreams come true, especially the ones that are scolded out of us. But Florian's done just that. I guess this magical being was walking on a different plane to me all along.

OR

Florian and I move the subject to the idea of the non-binary and his own fluidity. Is Florian clean cut in his two types of attraction? Florian is open, "I don't like to gender binarise people I'm attracted to these two types, *The Little Mermaid* and the *Johnny Bravo* types are just things I was introduced to as a child that I organically found myself attracted to. Now as an adult I have to re-educate myself to understand gender binary as it's not something you're exposed to. If Johnny Bravo had been female, would I have still been attracted to the masculine energy of the character? I don't think so. With the way times are evolving I feel because there's so much emphasis on this new way of looking at gender – and I mean this in a good way – I wouldn't want to not see myself giving a non-binary a person an opportunity to get to know them if I was single. I've not gone there yet, but the thought of it is *maybe* I would be. Interested, that is."

Sometimes I wonder whether the term bisexuality will be extinct in the future. This was a term that was founded on there being two genders to be attracted to. I think of that yoghurt in my fridge that I was waiting too long to eat: It's taken me so long to come to terms with the idea of being a bisexual that I worry it's a term that's *expiring*. This adds to my insecurity about it. I mean, does labelling myself as bi now sound backwards?! I can't tell if I've been overthinking again; I've been drinking too much tea as I've conversed with Florian, and I'm overloaded with caffeine. God I'm getting too old for tea. *God I'm getting too old to still be figuring myself out.*

Florian as ever isn't so bogged down. He says kindly, "Bisexuality hasn't even been given its spotlight in the modern era yet. It's okay."

We finish up the conversation to talk about his fantasy photo shoots. Florian loves to play dress up and his androgyny, his feminine side that was once shamed is now embraced by a whole community. His inner child has stayed with him, through childhood to Peter Pan at Disneyland to his own creations.

"When I was twenty-four, I went and bought a collectable Ariel doll and it was a big fat fuck you to my grandad!" He follows up quickly, laughing to himself, "And I *love* my grandad!"

I laugh at the idea of his prized doll sitting on his bedroom shelf, overseeing all of Florian's love conquests. He brushes his long blonde hair out of his face. "I've always been attracted to long hair, you know. And I love long hair on myself too. It's great! I'm in love with my*self* now too."

CHAPTER 3:
ORGANIC INCIDENTS

I'd never been a fan of Taylor Swift until I dated Mr Bojangles because that's how petty he made me. Suddenly, I understood why someone would write a ten-minute song about driving in a car with a guy you date for a few months who's just not that into you. Just like Taylor, it was an important lesson for me. I don't know how I hadn't had the realisation until my mid-twenties, but there I was, realising that I needed to love and value myself first or I'd give that power to others and be shattered if it worked out badly. I thought things had been going well, he told me he liked me, and I swear to God, he told me he wanted to be exclusive. Suddenly two months in he gets colder, more distant. Then one night he acts like the exclusive talk is a new conversation to be had, and that he'd never said anything of the sort. If we were to continue, we'd need to be non-exclusive for the time being. I wasn't ready for it to end, so I agreed to his terms. The next week he announced he was going on holiday with his ex. And you couldn't be mad, right Thomasin? Cos, you know, you agreed to being non-exclusive. But don't worry! He'll see you when he gets back. I was used to guys being mad at me or upset with me, but never totally disregard me and shag their ex with such unapologetic nonchalance that I cried so hard to a work colleague that I had a nosebleed. (This was back when I worked at Cutter & Squidge, and my colleague brought me a mountain of expiring chocolate balls to placate me as another mopped up the blood on my hands. I'm not sure I ever thanked them properly for that moment. Sometimes I think your colleagues see you have more meltdowns than your family.) I was so angry, and more at myself for how much I shrunk myself, how much I tolerated and how desperate I was to think I needed saving by a guy that really wasn't even right for me. It was humiliating; I was too old to be torn up about this. I had to wise up fast. I mentally shed a skin and killed all the parts of me that I didn't like so I could rebuild and turn myself into someone I could at least tolerate. I was kind of fuelled by fury. I absolutely *loathe* giving Bojangles credit for my personal growth, but his behaviour shocked me into looking at my life choices.

It's the same with standup comedy. The gigs that go badly are better for you because you learn something, even if it's just a simple, "Well I sure wasn't *their* cup of tea." I once did a gig that was so bad, dear reader, I'm still trying to figure out the lesson. It was at a pizza restaurant in Kent and the table layout was set out like a mediaeval banquet with no apparent stage. We had to either walk around the room giving our material to different tables or just stand in the one free corner. It was a closed event that people had paid tickets for, but they'd never been to live comedy in their life, and they all knew each other. Therefore, they took to heckling the MC and chatting when the acts were on. When the opening act did a, frankly, hilarious skit about giving a blow job to a guy with poor hygiene, the heckling turned to horrified silence. Then back to heckling, and the act, fed up with the whole vibe, heckled back. They made a joke about Brexit before realising the whole crowd were Conservatives who had voted Leave. I was up next, but not before the MC *told the crowd off* for their reaction.

"These people have come from very far to entertain you, so you need to listen to them!"

It was like a headteacher telling off the year group for laughing at the shoddy Theatre In Education tour that had come in to tell them through interpretive dance that smoking is NOT cool. While wearing Lycra. And sweating a lot. So, I went on to stony silence while cheerily pretending that everything was normal. I knew if I just got out my first punchline I could win them over, but as I did, the restaurant manager walked straight up to me (not onto the stage of course, over to the corner that I was performing in) and started GIVING ME ADVICE ON HOW TO HOLD THE MICROPHONE. And before I could try and banter with him to save the situation, he disappeared into the staff room. I looked at the crowd. They looked at me. It was over.

The next act to go on stormed it, and I looked at her like she was Jesus healing the lepers.

Wait, where was I? Ah yes, Mr Bojangles. When I dated him, I was introduced to all of these exciting parties and cool, unusual people. I was always holding him up on a pedestal; he was older than me (true), knew so much more than me (sort of), he was so much more liked than me (absolutely not). My only way to deal with the breakup was to try and beat him at all the things I'd initially admired about him. No way was I gonna experience all these interesting events as the anxious side piece and that be it. I kept showing up to stuff, becoming the life and soul of these parties, finding my way into expensive penthouse flats and private clubs and not paying a dime. Some of these cool, unusual people became my best friends. Several were from foreign countries, and I holidayed over Europe, staying in their homes. One of them even gave me a job. My life changed for the better after Bojangles because it opened up my world. And in the opening up of that world, I met Zain.

Zain loves threesomes. How do I know this, dear reader? Because he told me within five minutes of meeting him. Back when we were dating, Mr Bojangles took me to Shoreditch House to meet some of his party friends. Zain was one of them. Zain has a warm smile and big brown eyes, with dark curly hair styled to perfection. He's short but has a big energy, not in an overcompensating chihuahua sense but how you'd imagine those tiny stars like Lily Collins or

Bruno Mars would be. Or like a hobbit. On cocaine. I remember that night he was in a dapper suit, insisting that everybody try the espresso martini and getting us all absolutely plastered. At one point, he slid onto the sofa next to me and Mr Bojangles like a human embodiment of one sliding into your DMs. I cannot tell you how the conversation came up, but next thing I knew we were talking about the *Devil's three-way*.

"Most people think I'm straight," Zain says as we start our interview. And it's true; I certainly thought so. I remind him of our first conversation, of how the three of us sat on that sofa with our espresso martinis and how the conversation got sexual – in the way that it sometimes does when you're in a mixed group and relaxed and tipsy. You know, like when you play the drinking game Never Have I Ever? So, Zain brings up threesomes. Me, in my most unlikeable, performative way, tell Zain and Bojangles that, *"Of course* I'm open to threesomes. I like girls! Why wouldn't I share that with the guy? Ahahaha (kill me)." Zain pauses, then asks curiously, "What about with two guys?"

"Of course!"

"Really? Go on."

In all honesty, I don't remember much of how the conversation went after that. I just remember Zain's big brown eyes looking at me intently, asking more and more detailed questions until Bojangles hastily changed the subject.

Afterwards, on our way out together, I bring it up to Bojangles in the lift. "That was kind of funny how the conversation went so sexual, wasn't it? He's so wild!"

Mr Bojangles rolls his eyes, not looking at me. "Well no, not really. He brought up the *exact* same conversation when I brought a different a girl to one of his get-togethers."

The cogs start turning in my brain as the cogs of the lift wheel us down (I don't know how lifts work).

I put my hands to my face, feeling like an idiot. "Ohhhhhh he was *hitting on us.*"

"Yeah."

"I seeeee."

"Mmhmm."

Until Zain and I sat down for this interview, at the very same venue that we first met, we'd never discussed it. But as we sit at a table in Shoreditch House, I ask him if he remembers the conversation.

"I remember *every* conversation we've had," he says with a wink. Zain is a massive flirt. Now in his mid-thirties, he manages his own tech company, but his background was always in sales – which is pretty obvious. I sit down for the interview determined not to drink but within minutes I'm sold on the daiquiri, and by the time the interview is over, I'm pretty trolleyed on two daiquiris, an espresso martini and a shot of tequila. Zain is a natural salesman. And what is a salesman but a professional flirter?

But anyway, as I was saying, I concur with his self-assessment; I thought Zain was straight when I first met him. But after Bojangles pointed out that he was subtly inviting us to have a threesome, I figured he might be a bit bi. I just didn't know whether Zain knew it himself. So, I bring up that conversation. It wasn't a *hey here's a random topic of conversation teehee*, it was clearly a *let's steer the ship over HERE* kind of thing. Did he know what he was doing that night we first met? Zain nods.

"Yeah! Yeah, absolutely."

And it's in this moment that I know I've hit the jackpot in terms of the perfect interviewee, dear reader. Zain is shameless.

Zain was born to Sri Lankan parents who came over to the UK in their twenties. Born and raised in Royal Tunbridge Wells, *darling*, Zain had a middle-class upbringing. "I went to a private boy's school, so I was quite fortunate in that regard. It wasn't full boarding, my parents' excuse was always, 'we love you too much to send you away for full boarding.' Bullshit! They just weren't up for paying three times as much in fees! I had an amazing time there. Yes, there were elements of bullying but generally I didn't have any problems. I had a great childhood."

Sexuality-wise, Zain was always interested in girls and no one else. "It was a girl's school next door, and we had a fence separating our playgrounds. At lunchtime you would go over and chat to the girls at the fence. I was probably about sixteen when I met a girl through friends of friends. We had a bit of a flirty-flirty through the fence at lunch time. We exchanged numbers in the early days of texting on some sort of old Nokia – I think a flip phone!"

He and his crush, Anika, made plans to go on a walk on their lunch break. At that point they were in lower sixth and allowed to leave the premises on breaks. The trouble was, Zain completely forgot.

"As a boy I was playing football on our grounds. My phone was in my blazer! Anika was just left waiting for about an hour. Her entire lunch break." He shakes his head. "It's just one of those things where as a boy playing football you completely forgot! 'Cos it was like, 'Meet me tomorrow at lunch time' and it was like, 'Cool!' I didn't write it down or anything. So, lunchtime comes around and what do I do? What I always do! Play football."

That was Zain's first experience with the opposite sex. So far, so typical. We go on to talk about his impressions of boys.

"What I noticed was there was a mix of different people. Cool kids, sporty kids, the geeks. I was very much in the middle. Neither the brightest nor the dumbest kid. To put it in perspective, *everyone* was smart. But I was in the middle. So, I just kinda breezed through. But I noticed the cliques. I noticed the camp kids – I didn't know what camp was back then – but I certainly noticed the boys who we called gay. But throughout my entire schooling I was never interested in those guys, or any guys for that matter. I was happy dating women." When he remembered to go on the dates at least.

This experience was echoed at university. "Same thing! I went to gay bars with friends, I had lots of gay friends. But I saw it and thought, 'no.'"

Zain is open about his lack of understanding when he was younger. "What sounds ridiculous now is how to me it was you were either a gay guy, a lesbian or straight. I didn't understand anything else in between. There was a perception of what a gay guy is from celebrities to what I saw on TV."

Zain's bicuriousity bloomed later, beyond his teen years. At the age of twenty-two, he was looking at this university website and noticed a former school classmate was representing Wales on the rugby team.

"So, you can imagine, he was no longer the boy I knew at thirteen, he's now twenty-one, he's now 6ft 4 and ripped, shirtless. And I thought, 'Wow he's...you know,'" he gulps, "'grown into quite a handsome chap!' And I'm objectifying this man that I knew as a kid, but I quite *like* that I'm checking him out."

I ask if he was maybe confused about his thoughts but to Zain it was crystal clear. "I've seen lots of shirtless men from men's health magazines, whatever. It didn't do anything. This was a sexual thought. This was, 'I want to put my hands on these abs.'"

And what was Zain's follow up thought to these newly discovered sexual desires? Zain shrugs and remembers, "'Okay. Whatever!'"

Zain has never been on Grindr or any app equivalent, but he's had eight 'incidents' with men (a salesman always records his wins). A year after he first felt himself aroused by the photo of the rugby player, Zain was at a bar. At the time he worked in trade for a hospitality group, so it was his natural habitat. One of his girl mates found a stranger at the bar attractive, but this stranger was also with a male friend. Zain offered to go over with her.

"I love to wingman! Girls and guys, I love that."

And was ever a thought going through his head of, *but that person over there is a guy.* "Oh no, I'm just thinking I'm gonna chat, gonna have some banter."

I wonder how many bisexuals have disguised their sexual flirting as banter.

Me chatting you up in a bar? Banter.

Me putting a hand on your thigh? That's banter.

Me taking you into the same sex loos and shoving my hand down your crotch? That's banter, mate, don't be a bellend.

"I've been a salesman my entire career, it's pitching! In my head it was a little like, 'how do I make a sale, how do I close this for my own benefit and make it beneficial for my mate.' But I also went in for my own competition, my own gain."

Zain leads his friend over and starts to wingman, improvising as goes. "Hey boys, how you doing?" The men look up to see Zain stood there with his arms out, his girl mate trailing behind. "Look. I don't wanna be a dick," he says, which is a *great* way to start a conversation. He points to one of them and adds, "But my mate is really attracted to you." He turns to the other man and explains, "Not saying *you're* not a pretty boy – I have plenty of girl friends that would like you – but let me buy you a drink and let me tell you more."

Zain leans in proudly, waggling his eyebrows. "And you know what? He said yes." Closing his sale with a round of jaeger bombs, he boasts, "A communal drink that brings people together." (Although if by 'brings people together' he means bar fights, crying in the toilet to strangers and drunkenly attempting penetrative sex then I'd agree.) Zain chats to his chosen man all evening.

And what happened, dear reader, to Zain and this mystery man?! Did they go home together...?! Find out on the next page!!!

No.

But they became friends! And Zain agreed to meet up with this man on another night out. Did that second meeting make them realise and act on their sexual tension?! Quick, turn the page!

Also no.

In fact, Zain honestly just found a friend that night. But on their second meeting, when meeting his new friend's inner circle, he clocked a tall, handsome man with a muscular body. "He was a rugby-player-type, and he was bicurious!"

How did you know that?

Zain blinks and cocks his head at me as if it's obvious. "'Cos he told me."

I think back to our first conversation about threesomes. I laugh and ask if he tried the same conversation on Rugby Player Type Man. Zain is insistent that he was way more innocent at that time, "No! No, he just, we were having a chat! He asked how I met his friend, and I told him the story. And the guy's like, 'Huh. Interesting. By the way can I just say you're really well spoken, you're really worldly, and I'm very attracted to you. I hope that's not being too forward.' I was like no, tell me MORE!"

Zain describes two bicurious men circling each other flirtatiously as the evening went on. The initiation of their mutual attraction took some time to gain momentum. They tried a bit of side-stepping on the dance floor. "It was all very PC. It was just two men awkwardly dancing. Then we were like fuck it – let's go to the bar. We had three shots of tequila, we sat down and next thing I know he has his hand on my thigh. And that was it."

Fuelled with Dutch courage, they take an Uber back to Rugby Player's flat. Zain describes how even in the car they couldn't keep their hands off each other; touching, tumbling and ripping off each other's clothes while they eagerly ignore the Uber driver and the Uber driver eagerly ignores them back. He boasts, "It was everything you'd imagine it would be." Back at Rugby's flat, he and Zain spend the rest of the night "just having fun." Zain describes the vague conflictions at the back of his mind, "There were many points during where I'm thinking, '...What the hell am I doing?!' But then I'm also thinking, 'Oh my god I love your abs, oh my god I love your cock!'

"There were five or six points where I was like, 'What am I doing' and then I'm like, 'Screw it, this is amazing.' I'm having that conflict as I'm doing stuff. It's like, 'I'm kissing his thighs...I'm kissing his thighs! I haven't got to his cock yet but he's leading me there. Oh wow.'"

Zain gives an analogy, "It's like I'm getting to the peak of the mountain and I'm suddenly realising I have a stone in my shoe. It's irritating me, but is it *stopping* me?" He brings his daiquiri up to his mouth, hiding a devilish smile, "I'm not so sure."

Zain stayed the night but snuck out the next morning. Rugby Player Type Man followed up with a nervous text:

"Thanks for a lovely night, I really enjoyed it, do you wanna do something again but regardless...can we not tell our friends?"

Thus, the bisexual man retreats back into his hiding.

Armed with questions, Zain began conducting research, "I basically started googling bisexuality." You can't say technology hasn't helped people with this stuff.

"I was reading articles and watching porn, watching bicurious porn. And there was *bear*, there was *muscular*, there was *twink* and all of this world I was learning all about. And I'm still no expert but it's like, 'Okay where do I sit in here? And what am I attracted to – what do I like?' I didn't ever battle with it, I think, I just didn't know where I sat. I'm not a bear, I'm not a dom, I'm not a sub, I'm not a skinny little twink. And I'm not gay. I don't know where I sit. So why don't I just carry on with my," he puts his hands together, intertwining his fingers like a scheming villain, "...*research* and see what happens organically?"

Zain uses the word 'organic' about his incidents a lot. I think what he means to say is authentic. That or he's pronouncing the word 'orgasms' wrong.

"It's all organic. The only time it's manufactured," (I hope that's not a pun), "is that it's somebody that I've known and liked and I've *tried*. I go back to the example of when we had that conversation. It wasn't because in that moment I wanted a threesome then and there with you and Bojangles. Would I like to have experienced that opportunity or talked about it more? Maybe. But the scenario of having that conversation and leading to that point, yeah I would perhaps try to encourage or push.

"But it's not like I would go, 'Right! I want to suck a guy's dick! WHERE DO I GO TO DO THAT? Is it Twitter? Is it Google? How do I...?' I don't do that. I don't wake up thinking I'm going to do it. And partly, again," he lowers his voice, "this is partly where my moral compass does rightly or wrongly sway...I can be in a relationship with a woman, and yeah, the moment takes me, and I cheat on them with guys. And they don't know. And I've been in scenarios where I probably should not encourage it."

I ask Zain if he's ever cheated on women with other women. He smiles sheepishly. Do I detect the first glimmer of shame? "Yes. I have. So, it's not any different in that regard. It's the same. It comes back to the organic nature of my hookups with guys; if we were on a night out together and someone starts flirting with me, of course I can say no and I'm not going to do anything and then I go home. And I do that," he sees my face and his voice goes unbelievably high as he stresses, "*99.9% of the time!* You know? But there are times where I'm in that moment and I do want to have that, and I have it. And so," he interrupts himself to flirt with the Italian waitress who is covered in tattoos and bringing us more booze, "I love your tattoo!"

She smiles and replies, "Thank you! My friend is a tattoo artist and I tell him with my body, he can do as much as he wants!"

We get sidetracked by the Italian accent and booze and Zain tells me the story of a secretly gay Italian man who was fiercely Catholic – to the point where he had a massive cross tattooed on his stomach. We discuss the juxtaposition of someone devoted to a church that hasn't exactly had the friendliest connections to the LGBTQ community.

"He was like, 'I don't want you to cum in my mouth,' and I'm like okay but I'm gonna cum on your body and he said, 'Yeah.' So I was aiming for the tattoo of the cross! I was fucking aiming for it! I was standing there like I'm going to fucking nail this. It's terrible! But that was my own game! 'The irony is not lost on me here, FRANCISCO!'"

We settle back to our previous topic. "So, for me, everything is organic. It's never pre-planned and," Zain holds out his hands admittedly, "You know, cheating is cheating. I'm no angel. But there's a difference between having a long-term affair or actively pursuing something. Everything that has happened to me has been organic."

Zain is currently in a relationship with a woman where she's highly aware of her partner's bicuriousity, and if anything fuels it. "In our early days of our relationship we sexted about it. We started with an open relationship, we encouraged it. She was getting off with guys and I was getting off to it."

I initiated this interview with Zain because I know vaguely of one of his 'incidents' that happened a few years ago. Something that happened when he was with the girlfriend that he's still with now.

It's as tense as a moment in the show *Dragon's Den*. I sit back and ask my salesman, but I've already looked at the numbers and heard his pitch. I already know the answer.

"Does she know?"

"She does not know."

And he does not want to tell her. So, he tells me instead.

Zain describes a wedding venue, an incredible manor with a labyrinth of rooms. "There are literally thousands of castles in France. And this wedding was at this beautiful castle. It was small, but it was, you know, it was a castle! It was my friend's wedding. My partner was a plus one. I was at the bar ordering a whisky when she caught the bouquet."

Zain shows me a video on his phone capturing an incredible moment. The camera, recorded by a friend of his, follows the bride throwing her bouquet aggressively, a young woman grabbing it and the room cheering and screaming her and Zain's names in delight. The camera quickly pans over to Zain at the bar, his back to the ruckus but clearly knowing what it all means. He looks over at the camera with a tired expression, lifting his arm in the air and gestures to the room, mouthing, "Shots?"

"All the bridesmaids' partners are buying me commiseration shots." (Haha it's so funny to joke about how men hate marrying the women who love them hahahaHAHAHAHA-HAHA). "And I met this guy at the bar when I was having some quiet time to myself. We got chatting and I realised he was the father of the Maid of Honour, Paul. He says, 'My commiserations.' We did a shot together and we were just chatting. He was married, apparently not happily."

"How do you know that?" I ask.

He blinks again. "Because he said!"

"We just got chatting as guys do. 'Been married a time, we're still together for convenience and the family.' His daughter is there, and I say she looks beautiful but then I say, 'Hang on, she's like, what? Thirties?' He said, 'Yes, thirty-one.' I said, 'To be fair, mate, you look forty. You look young, you look fit!'"

I can concur after seeing the photo of Paul that he did indeed look fit. He looks like Lindsay Buckingham from Fleetwood Mac, circa the late 90s.

"And he said, 'Oh thank you, I'm fifty-two. I had my daughter quite young.' And he's going all easy-breezy like, 'I try and keep fiiiit, I work out a loooot, I've got a home gyyyym.' He said, 'To be honest, it's a bit of a release for me. I want to claim back my masculinity – and frankly I'm just horny all the time. But I can keep up with the guys in cross fit!'"

I tell Zain like a gossipy neighbour, "Oh he *so* wanted you to know that."

Zain laughs. "Yeah, yeah, yeah! And I was like '…okay.'"

I ask him if he was aware what was happening? "No! I was like whatever, we were talking about his daughter a minute ago and bearing in mind my partner is here!"

Paul invites Zain out for a cigarette. Zain holds up his empty whisky glass and Paul leans over the bar, grabbed a bottle of whisky and off they go – but not before Zain tells his girlfriend he's going outside for a drink. She pecks him on the cheek.

"We just sat on this ledge on this old beautiful castle drinking some whisky. And then out of nowhere he said, 'I just – I just need to like, loosen up a bit!'"

Paul takes off his jacket to reveal a white, tight shirt. He and Zain lock eyes. For a moment it looks like he's going to make a move. Instead, Paul drops to the ground and starts doing press ups.

"I was like, 'What are you doing?!' And he said, 'I just had some built-up energy and you don't want that,' and I said, 'What do you mean?' and he said, 'I'm really horny.' I said, 'Oh, okay. Um, why don't you go do something about

75

that…?' He said, 'Why, are you offering?' And I was like, 'I meant you should – Sorry – WHAT?'"

Paul apologises but persists. He's turned on. He thinks Zain is hot. And he's clearly aware that there's some part of Zain that likes him back.

"And I'm like, 'What the fuck is happening?' And the next thing you know I'm saying, 'Well let me have a feel!' So, I cop a feel. He enjoys it. And I say," he mimes looking both ways to check the coast is clear, "'would you like me to suck you off?! ''Cos you can't go back in looking like that!'" He says, pointing to Paul's obvious boner.

They're outside the castle, round the corner from where the guests are. It's quiet. So, they venture further round the side where Zain pushes him up against the wall and does what he says. They don't kiss.

Surely Zain was scared he was going to get caught? "There was always that risk, but I thought it's gonna be a quickie." He smirks down at me and raises his shoulders faux-modesty, "I'm pretty good babe! What can I say? Maybe it was risky, I don't know. We just had that little moment."

Zain and Paul finish, pour a couple of drinks and say, "Weeeell that was wonderful. Thank you!" They exchanged numbers but Zain knew it was over. "My fucked up moral compass says, 'No. I'm not going to go somewhere deliberately to see you. There's already too many risky scenarios there.' And I'm not attracted to anything preconceived."

And how did Zain freshen up before returning to normality at the party? "I washed my mouth out with fifteen-year-old whisky straight from the bottle and asked the hotel for a toothbrush."

"What a slaaaag," I say, slurping down my martini. The shamelessness is catching.

And then he heads back into the party like nothing had happened. His girlfriend was out on the dance floor, swinging the bouquet, having the time of her life.

Like Florian, Zain appears to be very in control of his bisexual identity. There appears to be only one 'incident' where he was out of his depth.

"I was in Kuwait on a work trip. It's a dry country; no alcohol anywhere. It's not like Dubai. You can't drink in five-star hotel bars, you just can't get it – unless you're the royal family. It's strict and backwards. I was in a hotel on my own. I wasn't allowed an unmarried woman to stay with me, I can't have a guy – homosexuality is forbidden. I thought there's no way *anything* is gonna happen on this trip." To distract himself from his horniness he did what one naturally does and went scuba diving.

la la la
I'm not horny
la la la

"When I got back I thought, 'Fuck it,' I'm going to the hotel spa – it's being paid for by the company. I'm getting a facial!"

The hotel informed him of a special full body massage which Zain decided to book in. "The massage therapist was a guy. Again, because of all the strict rules it *had* to be a man that did it. So, I'm wearing these tiny mesh shorts and he's giving me the full massage."

Zain is on a marble lined table in the main room. He describes a separate room where he would be dried off, and then further back was a locker room.

"He locked the rooms for privacy reasons. So, I'm standing there in my towel, getting…dried off." Back in the present, Zain raises his shoulders looking bashful. "Then he was on his knees going around *that* area. I later found out what he was doing was testing the waters. He was a closeted gay man living in a country where homosexuality was outlawed.

He was rubbing up there and massaging and looking up at me and I know that this is a WORK TRIP?!" He suddenly explodes, "I could go to prison! *If I get a boner I am going to prison!*

"And I'm looking around and you know, obviously you're fighting it, and he's getting right in there! And then he softly said, 'It's okay, you can relax. I've locked the door.' And I said, 'Uh?'" Zain describes how out of nowhere this massage therapist starts grabbing him. Zain says something along the lines of, "Uhhhhh…" The masseuse asks, "Is this okay? I want to satisfy you." Zain replies, "*Uhhhhh…*"

The masseuse apologises and explains himself. He's twenty-four and from Algeria. He's gay. He's in a foreign country working for money and all he does is massage "ugly, old fat men." He thinks Zain is beautiful and he wants to have some fun. "And the next thing I know I'm just standing there, in this spa getting a reaaaally good blow job 'cos I'm probably the first blow job he's done in a while. He's grateful, I'm grateful." It was like he was Cinderella and for one night he got to go to the ball…s. "And he goes, 'One second,' and he unlocks the door, goes out and tells the staff that he will close up for the evening. He comes back and goes, 'The spa is closed.' I go, 'Okay.' He locks the door again, puts me back on the marble table and climbs on it. I'm so confused, I'm so turned on, I'm so scared by the risk."

They spend an hour in the spa together, ending up in the hot tub. "I was like, 'am I…*paying extra* for this service?! Do

I still tip you after? Do you want money? Do I…are you an escort? What do I DO?!'"

But there wasn't any payment for the moment. It was an organic incident. Like with Paul. They parted ways and Zain found himself panicking alone in his hotel room.

"I freaked out a little bit afterwards, like are there cameras, will I get arrested, will someone knock on my doors? I didn't tell anyone. I just internalised it and I had to get to work. And then I came home. I've told three people, Thomasin. You're the third."

It's a wild story and it puts things into perspective. Zain and I have the option to explore whatever we want in our country, regarding our bisexuality. Granted, people in the UK still experience homophobia and we must remain vigilant to things moving in the right direction, but we're never (hopefully) going to go to prison for our antics. Dear reader, it's bizarre to say this but it truly is a privilege to be held back by our own insecurities, and no one else's. I'm aware that Zain's stories don't necessarily undo the common notion that all bisexuals are sexually promiscuous, but my god do I now more than ever see the liberation in that.

I ask Zain if he'd ever be open with his parents about his sexuality. Zain contemplates. "No is the answer," he says after a while, "probably not. My sisters know. But there's still a big stigma in Asian culture and some people in our family *have* broken that." He pauses and adds, "And a lot haven't."

"They haven't been ostracised, but the family essentially are not as comfortable as if it were a straight couple. I'm very supportive of it. I just think the people that know just don't necessarily talk about it much. It's brushed under the carpet like, whatever."

I think of Rugby Player Type Man. I think of Paul the Wedding Guest. I think of him asking me and Bojangles, a stranger and acquaintance in equal measure, about threesomes. I tell Zain that from what I've heard of his story, it doesn't seem like he's seeking a man to bring back home to the family anyway.

Zain nods in agreement. "And this is the important thing. I think there's a difference between bicuriosity and bisexuality. Traditionally, bisexual is someone who is attracted to both girls and guys and *my* definition is someone who wants to *date* them. The thing is, if you're bisexual then you should want to have a boyfriend or a girlfriend. You're open to relationships with any gender. I don't want a relationship with a guy."

I ask if he's ever been in love with a guy. The answer comes fast and sure. "No. I've never thought of a guy that way, I've never been on a date with a guy! It has all been sexual, it has all been flirty and it has all been fun. And if it gets any more than that, I'm not interested." Because of this, Zain doesn't feel he needs any coming out story. "I don't need to tell any member of my family about me sucking a dick."

Zain doesn't necessarily feel like he's the right person for this book; Zain loves women. He wants to date women. He wants to get married to a woman and have kids with a woman. "I've never gone up to a guy that is straight and gone, 'Can I suck your dick,'" I raise an eyebrow and he quickly adds, "...sober."

He continues. "Every single scenario has involved alcohol, a night out, serendipity, the circumstances being right. Or if I'm not with a girlfriend or I'm not at a party that I'm enjoying myself in. 'Cos when I'm out with friends I'm out with friends, I'm not trying to get laid. I think I'm a wrong case study in that regard. The success ratio has been high but the number has been low."

Zain doesn't like penetrative sex with men either. "It's just not been fun for me. And when I've done it to someone, I've just not been into it in the same way. For me, I love sucking dick. I love it from the power standpoint, the pleasure standpoint. A guy getting head from a girl, they think it's a power position for them. But actually, you as the girl giving the pleasure – *you* are the powerful one. 'Cos when I'm with a guy who's 6' 4" and 110kg and I'm in control of this man? Well, that's really all I wanna do."

By now I'm pretty drunk. We ask for the bill and chat about meeting up again soon. Zain is *very* keen to meet my boyfriend. I tell Zain how he reminds me of that quote, apparently attributed to Oscar Wilde but who the fuck knows who really said it.

Everything is about sex except sex. Sex is about power.

One might feel like James Bond or Villanelle from *Killing Eve* when saying that quote, but unfortunately, I'm so drunk my Essex twang comes out and I slur my words to babble:

Errythin is abaht sssex. 'Ceptsex. Sex? Is abaht powaaaah

The bill has arrived. I clumsily search my pockets for my debit card but Zain snatches the bill away for himself.

"Absolutely," he smiles. "Sex. Money. Power. You know it's wrong to have those three categories? Because sex *is* money. Sex *is* power. Power isn't always sex, and money isn't always power. But sex is both. And that's what I love."

CHAPTER 4:
THE PROPOSAL

"Wait," I say, "just so I understand – this was at a party?"

"Nope. It wasn't at a party," Danni replies pointedly. "It was a public space." Someone walks by the door and we pause, busying our papers for the photocopier to look like we're working. Danni then continues, "Yeah, it wasn't at a party; it was at a public space."

"Okay, so *where*?" I ask.

"A public space."

"Like a train station?"

"A *public space*. That's all you need to know. A public space. It was not a space that would be open to that behaviour. Okay?"

It's five years ago. Danni and I are standing by a photocopier on a lazy Saturday morning and we're bickering over the details of a very interesting New Year's Eve that she's just had. Danni's always got the best stories, but like some kind of public relations specialist, she's always omitting certain details to protect herself. Danni doesn't work in public relations, though. She's now a research scientist and bettering the planet with all kinds of...erm, research. But right now, it's five years ago, she's still a year away from graduating from her masters and I'm still hoping that I'll get my big break in a West End show. So, we're both lowly temps for the admin office of a local GP centre. I'm living in Lewisham in a house share with a fifty-five-year-old Christian woman, a Nigerian IT expert and an Italian chef. It should be a sitcom but instead we never see each other and we're all desperately depressed. That or they're all hanging out without me. Danni's living at home with her mum, her sister ("I love her") and brother ("He's an arsehole"). She's a couple of years younger than me but acts like the big sister; she's my lifeline in this job.

She continues the story, "It was quite early in the night 'cos I was meeting a friend later on. So, I went somewhere else after."

But I'm still wondering what the hell she means by public space. We walk back from the photocopying room back towards the office, passing through the now vacant patient waiting area. I gesture around us, "I mean, did you do it *here*?"

She snaps, "I'm not telling you where I was! But it was a public space where it would not have been acceptable...for two women to go to...anyway that's what happened and then I left. And *she* came out all dishevelled, all like 'oh my god that was the best experience.'" Danni smirks and adds, "The best part is that the particular girl I was with was a stud lesbian, right? Very butch, very masculine. And *I* topped her."

I cackle, and it echoes down the empty hallway. I roll my eyes and praise the skies all at once. "*Of course* you did." Of course she did. Because she's Danni Campbell.

Danni's much cooler than me. She's intelligent, gorgeous and knows how to look after herself. She's a few years younger but so ahead of her years ("that's what trauma will do to you"). She's a fighter. Even as we skip ahead to the present, five years from that memory, the twenty-seven-year-old Danni still seems to be facing the world with a meta-phorical baseball bat. Life has hurled many things her way: death, violence, a heavy flow. And she's batted it right back with ferocity, and then slut dropped for good measure to show everybody that it wasn't all that difficult and also that she's very sexy. She sometimes reminds me of Mel B – picture Scary Spice in a lab coat.

But she's also more than that. She's gentle, self-deprecating and compassionate. She's an old colleague that I regret not keeping in touch with. But we're here now, in an extremely loud pub on a Friday night, sitting at a wonky table with goldfish bowl sized glasses of gin. "I can't drink too much tonight, I'm going to a shibari class tomorrow."

"A *shibari class*?"

"Oh," Danni says, setting down her drink like she's about to tell me about the birds and the bees, "shibari is— "

"I know what it is!" I insist childishly. We've already drifted back into our big sister / little sister dynamic.

Do you know what shibari is, dear reader? If you're next to your phone, why not Google it? We'll wait. And if you're on an aeroplane, public transport or anywhere without signal, why not ask the person sitting next to you? It will be a great conversation starter!

Okay, have you Googled it / asked a stranger? Good. Now get back to reading my book, you distracted slut.

The pub is incredibly loud. It's a Friday night and there's a group of lads having the time of their life on the table over from us. It's hard to hear Danni over there whooping and cheering. "I'm an enthusiast of kinky spaces."

"You're an enthusiast of Kevin Spacey?!"

"No!"

It's difficult to have a private conversation about BDSM when we're yelling at each other over a small, lopsided table, but Danni doesn't seem bothered with who hears, and she lays it out to me as if it's the results of her scientific research.

"I'm 100% a switch. I've found I'm 70% a sub, but I do have my moments." I see a lad from the other table double take and glance our way as if he's thinking, 'Did I hear that right?' I tuck my chair closer into the wonky table, as if that will help. Danni pays it no mind, but she hasn't always been this confident.

"I was extremely shy when I was younger. Especially when it came to sex. I was very aware of it from a young age, but I was never actually sexually *liberated* you know? I was almost eighteen when I lost my virginity and only because I was terrified that it wasn't legal! I was scared of breaking the rules."

Danni's first boyfriend was a short-lived affair with a boy she was studying with. "I lost my virginity and told my mum the next day because I am that person. She almost crashed the car and she started to cry. She was in the middle of telling me a story and I blurted out, 'I SLEPT WITH HIM' and then screeeeech! And she was doing that typical mum wavy hands flapping at her face as she cried. And I was just like," she turns her chair to address her invisible mum in a calm voice, "'Please don't crash the car, don't cry. Please. It happened.' And that was that."

She turns back to me as if she's a newscaster reporting back to the live studio. She solemnly repeats, "And that was that."

I wonder how her mum would feel if she were to know about Danni's bisexuality. Danni's thoughtful. She tells me about a story last summer at a family barbeque. Her brother had just gotten engaged, and around the table where Danni was sitting next to her mum, her godmother asks Danni about her dating life. "So, what about you? You know, are you seeing anyone?" Incidentally, Danni tells her no but is actually lying – she's seeing a guy who is at that very barbeque and currently helping himself to a plate of sausages. (I'm slightly relieved to know I'm not the only person she hides stuff from). "So she goes, 'So you're not seeing anyone? Any guys?' I say no and she suddenly says, 'Any women?' This threw me because I don't know how she *knew*."

"Maybe you told her when you were drunk?"

"I mean, may*be*!"

Danni was sure that if her godmother knew then she would have told her mum. "But trust me, my mum does not know." So, what's the deal? Danni thinks back to her cousin's wedding, an event prior to the barbeque. "I was really drunk. I do remember sneaking off to have a cigarette with her so I'm thinking maybe I shared secrets, then? It was awkward because I had this gut reaction when she asked." It's as if she's been punched in the stomach, her eyes widening, "*NooOOoooo!*"

Danni's godmother read the situation immediately and has not asked Danni about it since, which Danni is more than okay with, but we'll talk more about her family later.

Danni met her second boyfriend, Ryan, on the dating site *Plenty of Fish* at the age of eighteen. Ryan introduced her to the world of BDSM.

"He was older than me. Well, he was *quite a bit* older than me." She then interrupts her own sentence to argue with herself, "Well not 'quite a bit' but…I was eighteen and he was twenty-eight."

"I believe the unit of 'quite a bit years' is actually ten years."

"Shut up."

Barely an adult, Danni recalls putting her own sexual pleasure on the back burner to please Ryan. "I just wanted to make him feel as good as possible. It's all I knew from porn. it's all I knew from everything which is that it's all about the man. And when the man finishes it, it's DONE. But I loved it. I thrived off that kind of stuff."

Danni discovered that she enjoyed being submissive, but there were certain parts that she didn't enjoy. "He introduced me to that world and that space and that was great. But he was the wrong kind of dom because he was not a dom, he was just somebody who wanted sexual gratification and wanted to give nothing back. That's what a dom is. And in my mind, I was like, Oh my God, he's just a dominant. But it's *not it at all.* And this is not the theme of your book, I know, but the point I'm making is he was NOT a dom, actually. He was just a guy who wanted to have sex with women who'd only pleasure him."

I shake my head. "I mean, hiding behind the BDSM scene to disguise the fact that you're selfish in bed, that's not great."

Danni nods. "Yes! You're selfish in bed!"

"Stop kink shaming me!" I yell back, pretending to be Ryan. I mean what a get out of jail card, dear reader!

"It's ridiculous," Danni says. "It's *ridiculous.* That's not a kink, you're just a bastard! Just say it! 'I'm a bastard, that's my kink!'"

So where does bisexuality come into play in this story?

Danni explains. "What I will take from the experience is that I learned my limits. I learned what I didn't like in bed, which I'm extremely thankful for, because there will always be that part of human curiosity where I'd be like, well, 'I could *try* this.' Well, I've tried it! And I know there won't be these detrimental barriers in the future, for future partners. But ultimately, what I will also be thankful for is that he opened my mind and opened that level of discussion about women. Of other women."

For Danni, Ryan was the first person to tell her not only was it alright that she was attracted to women, but it was something to be celebrated.

"But I guess, following on from the selfish comments about him, he wanted to see two women in his bed. That was it. It wasn't about me at all, or exploring who I was. But while I'm thankful for that, he opened my mind to even talking about it, because I was so afraid. It was such a re-pressed feeling." She stops and picks up her drink, sighing at the memory and repeating, "*It was such a repressed feeling. And again, this is gonna sound really bizarre. Erm. Erm.*" She suddenly stalls like a car, getting shy. She giggles.

"What?!" I stage whisper, leaning over the wonky table. I get my sleeves wet.

"Okay, so...*You* know what you think about when you masturbate and you orgasm. And that's your private thoughts. They don't get shared with aaaanybody else. Right?" I start giggling too and she points at me like I'm evidence. "EXACTLY!" She declares to an imaginary jury (a couple of lads on the table next to us look over again). "And that's exactly it because you're like, 'Oh, shit.' Because you go red, you go embarrassed because they're *your* thoughts! Right? That's the sort of same level of thoughts I had when I thought about women. It was all about my very, very, VERY private thoughts! So, the fact that somebody is trying to say to me, 'Oh, it's okay for you to have a very, very pri-vate thought and bring it publicly to me.' I'd never felt that comfortable doing that. I mean, I *still* don't feel comfortable about that, like, my thoughts have shifted! And I'm still not sharing them even with the current person I'm dating. I never share that stuff. They're *my* thoughts." I can relate. I recall my own first (and insanely jealous) boyfriend at nineteen asking what I thought about when I masturbated. I panicked, trying to think of the most feminine and unthreatening thing, so I said, "Uh. Flowers. Flowers in a field." Idiot.

Danni was liberated, being able to be open for the first time in her life about how much she loved women, but what this did was open the floodgates for Ryan's own fantasies, which quickly took over.

"He'd say, 'What kind of women would you like to see?' And then he kind of quickly retracted that because he was like, 'these are the women *I* want to see!'"

As a result, Dani became defensive. "He'd show me pictures or point out women in the street, 'Oh, what do you think of her?' I'd think, 'None of your fucking business!' Even if I like this woman, I'm not going to tell you because you're just going to be like," she makes a similar noise to one of the excited lads at the table over from us, "'WAHEEEY!'"

I can sadly relate. I recall a boyfriend who knew about my bisexuality, and when we'd watch a film or TV together and I remarked on how gorgeous a woman was, his first response would be, "Would you lick her out?" And I can't tell you how much of a turn off that is, dear reader. I mean I know it should be the opposite, but I'm a prude at heart, I really am! I don't want to imagine going down on her right this very second. Aaargh let me take her out for a coffee first! Danni nods. "It completely destroys every element of it, it irritates me *so* much. But it's like, the worst thing a guy could do. And I'm really fortunate now I'm not, you know, I'm not in that space where I'm around people who think like that. I'm so lucky, you know? Because honestly, there were so many guys who were like that."

It's funny, because I worry whether my prudish nature is evidence for the fact that actually maybe I'm not as attracted to women as I think I am, but Danni disagrees. "I like a woman's aesthetic and I like how they are and I want to get to know them. Without going into too much detail, when it comes to sex with me, I need to know the person – I don't do one-night stands. I don't do casual one-offs."

I look at her, slack jawed, and ask, "What about that stud lesbian on New Years that you topped?"

"That was different."

"What about that guy on the New Years *before* that?" (Danni has a habit of hooking up with people on New Year's.)

"I still met him before – I met him twice before that happened!" she replies indignantly. "I don't just do one night stuff with strangers. I don't. It just stresses me because I'm like, 'I don't know you! Why should I trust you?' For me, sex is such a sacred thing. So, if I'm walking down the street and I see a woman that's attractive and my partner's like, 'Oh, would you lick her out?' I'm like, 'Sorryyyyyy. Sir? SIR?! I do not know this woman. I have never met this woman in my life.' Yeah. It's so silly. And the thing is, if that makes someone bicurious instead of a bisexual, it's still valid! But the thing that gets me upset, unfortunately, is that bisexual is this horrible *fence* that you sit on. You're not accepted by anybody. So, boyfriends have said, 'Ooooh great we can have a threesome at some point' and then like, gay women don't want anything to do with you! I've had women say, 'Oh so you're not a lesbian' and correct – I'm not! I like men too." With all these complications, it gets me wondering: maybe the stereotype of bisexuals being sluts are just because those are the bisexuals that have the most success? Like if you're being a total slag (and please know I write that as a compliment) then eventually you'll get through all the awkwardness and get some actual sex – with men *and* women! For people like Danni and I, it seems like our lack of experience comes from our (lack of) approach to casual sex. We get left on that fence!

Danni quickly outgrew Ryan, finding that although he was older, he wasn't taking care of her emotionally or physically in the way she had hoped. Even the way they broke up Danni found to be extremely immature. "We both ghosted each other! I mean I was eighteen, but he was twenty-eight, if he's ghosting me at that age then that's a bit sad, isn't it?"

Getting the timing right for bisexuals dating one another can be hard, as Danni finds. I suppose it's similar to the rest of the LGBTQ community, one person may be further along in their journey, whether it's self-acceptance, acceptance from their family or even if they're in the right location.

As a teenager, Danni found herself enjoying rock climbing where she was really good friends with a girl called Lara. Lara was beautiful, head to toe in tattoos, and very much in love with Danni.

"She was bisexual as well. She would always flirt with our male instructor. He was very cautious because a lot of people he taught were underage so he'd be like, 'AS THE WITNESSES CAN SEE, I'M JUST GOING TO MOVE YOUR LEG INTO THE HARNESS NOW.' He was American," she adds, as if that explains it. "And she's just there like, 'Help me with my harness' and spreading her crotch in his face. And everyone's laughing and he was just like, 'Eurgh!'" For a moment I mentally applaud the American instructor for being one of the good ones, then Danni follows this up by saying, "They ended up in this weird, long-distance relationship, actually. For a bit." Oh.

They lived close to each other, and Danni found comfort at Lara's home. "She had an Italian mother with these massive nana arms, always making pasta. It was just so nice. Sometimes Lara would come home, and I'd already be there in the kitchen with her mum making the sauce. She didn't even know I was coming!"

Danni was only fifteen when they met, but as she grew up and started experimenting, she realised Lara was into the kinky scene like her.

"Lara was a bit older than me."

"Are we talking 'quite a bit older' units?" I interrupt.

"No, just three years, but when you're seventeen and she's twenty, that's a lot. I looked up to her."

Lara's dad was extremely homophobic. "Like, extremely. He absolutely loved me but he didn't love her. It was weird. He knew she was seeing women and seeing men. Even her mum was rather reserved about it, but Lara never shied away from it. She's confident with all her tattoos while her dad's a strict Catholic." Although, as I recall Francisco from Zain's escapades, those two things don't have to be exclusive.

It seems that he couldn't wrap his head around the idea of Lara choosing women to date when she could also opt for men – a more traditional, and more widely accepted path. "He'd ask her 'Why? Why are you doing this?' And she'd be like, 'It's done! By the way, here's my girlfriend.' She didn't give a shit. They had a turbulent, turbulent relationship. But he loved me. He was like, 'You're my daughter!' And I'd say, 'Erm, you have a daughter.' And he'd say, 'No, no, *you're* my daughter!' They saw me as just her mate, not a girlfriend. And I was! I just kissed her twice, that was it."

"Wha – wait – like with tongue?"

Danni bursts out laughing. "What are we, twelve?! '*With tongue?*'"

"No, no, I'm just trying to understand, are we talking about the way Italians air kiss on the cheek or whatever, you know!" I flap, going red.

But no, they snogged twice. With tongue. Danni spends a while searching for the memory of the first time. Danni was tipsy but she wasn't sure where. "I think we were out. No. Were we at hers?"

She thinks. A lightbulb goes off. "Oh! We were at her girlfriend's house."

"Oh, *Danni*."

"But her girlfriend knew!"

Lara and her girlfriend at that time were going through a very on-off relationship, and this was at a particularly off moment. Lara had been Danni's biggest opener to understanding who she was, after Ryan. But Lara wanted to be more than that, confessing she was in love with Danni. "I said, 'No, you're not. You're lonely. You're a bit bored and you miss your ex.' And she said, 'No, I do love you and here are all the reasons I'm in love with you…'"

Lara's outpouring of love was the first time Danni had experienced romantic love coming from a woman. She'd thought about it, she'd fantasised about it, she'd wanted it. But how did she react?

Well, something on par with my rose gifting speech.

"'Okay. BUT! LIAR. Ahhhh. Hehehehe. No homo!'"

So, in short, she freaked out. Did Danni just not feel the same way?

"I really tried to keep it as platonic as possible," she explains. "I was super attracted to her. I loved her. But the thing is, I was not ready to come out of my shell and say, 'I'm dating a woman.' I was so young, I was still so very much closeted. I was still finding out more about myself whereas she was full-fledged, holding hands with girls in public, not giving a shit. But I wasn't there yet. I wasn't that person. Which is funny because nowadays when dating women, I realise I'm the more open one!"

Lara and Danni stayed friends, but it continued to be messy. "I went off to uni so I'd only ever come home occasionally to cook pasta sauce with her mother and that. What also complicated things was that I got engaged at nineteen."

"WHAT. To who?!" I realise more and more that there is so much that Danni hasn't told me about her life.

"Oh, someone I met at uni. Lara was actually over to stay and we went to an indoor rock climbing centre, and this guy was there climbing by himself and he kept looking at us. So, I went up to him and said, 'Stop staring.' And he said, 'Oh, I'm sorry, I'm just new to the area, I'm a tourist. I'm not good at making friends.' And push came to shove, at the end of the day, and we, er, we got engaged."

"Wait, no. I feel like you skipped a bit there."

"Oh, I skipped *a lot*," she says, sitting there cooly with her arms crossed. I look at her. She looks at me.

"Would you care to elaborate?"

So, Danni and this young Canadian man, we'll him call Dash, had a long-distance relationship for about a year. They were the same age and in between university breaks, he'd come over to stay with Danni. They were together for around six months when he proposed. "My gut told me it was coming. We were watching that film *The Proposal* with Ryan Reynolds and Sandra Bullock – it's one of my favourites. Sandra Bullock's character is Canadian too. And I was like, 'Okay, cool. I know what's happening here.' Dash pauses the film at the part where Ryan Reynolds proposes to Sandra Bullock, then he gets down on one knee and he's got this ring and I'm like," she grits her teeth, "'Oh that's loooovely, that's greeeeat.' But even in my head I was thinking, 'I don't know this guy very well, but it's a long engagement. I can have an engagement for two years. It's *fine*.'" But it never got to two years.

Danni rolls her eyes at the memory. "Yeeeeah six months later I took the ring off like, 'Yeah, you're a liability, get out my face.'"

I splutter over my second goldfish bowl of gin, "*Danni!*"

"Well, no I didn't say it quite like that I was just like," she puts her hand on the table and mimes pushing the engagement ring out of the way like it's a new food she's tried, "'This isn't for me. So goodbye.'"

Danni never told Dash about her bisexuality, but in fact had her own suspicions that he was perhaps gay.

"Why? Did he like butt stuff?" I say, sounding like a twelve-year-old again.

"Well, here's the thing he was *so* against that stuff, he didn't want anything to do with that. But he didn't have sex with me until three months in. For three months we slept in the same bed and nothing. I laid out on a platter for him and NOTHING. For three months it was bloody celibate! But then I caught him in the toilet with a men's muscle magazine! And he weren't on the toilet, do you know what I mean?"

"Maybe he was reading about protein and gains," I giggle.

"I mean, there's only so much protein you can read about before you're trying to expel it into a toilet. You know?"

"*Jesus Christ.*"

"There was a lot there's a lot going on there. Yep." She takes a big gulp of her drink.

"Well, that kind of makes sense now why he wanted to watch *The Proposal*," I say dreamily, thinking of the handsome Ryan Reynolds.

Danni's next long-term relationship was with a man. They were together for several years, but ultimately it didn't work out. Danni has a feeling he was intimidated by her budding career while he was still living at home trying to make it as a Twitch streamer. When she found herself single again, she headed to the dating apps.

"After about two weeks of having my preferences to men, I thought I need to take this opportunity to really look at my options here, before I get back into a serious relationship. And that's the most important thing. It really made me really re-evaluate what I actually wanted. So, I looked at the women's section and I realised, a lot," she hesitates, "*a lot* of the issues I was having when it came to dating and speaking to women, was honestly that they had a lot of hang ups, a lot of issues, mental health issues where they were just bicurious and wanted somebody who was safe. And I already had a lot of that with men anyway. Me being a safe space for them. The guy I'd just broken up with, for years I was the only source of happiness for him, and I don't want that. I want to be equal, and I want to be looked after too. I was searching desperately for a woman who wasn't damaged in some way. And it sounds really harsh to say – and I'm not saying I don't have my own issues – but I was really looking for somebody who was just willing to open up and explore. I wanted a Lara."

Danni's never had a particular type when it comes to women, as long as they look completely different to herself. "Some people date their twin but I'm not that person. Like I might go for someone with a boyish frame and smaller boobs, or maybe someone with much wider hips and taller than me."

Danni met a Swedish girl, Maria. "Maria was so attractive, tall, blonde, blue-eyed. Really slight and sort of androgynous but she had these big hips. I loved her energy, she was super bubbly. It wasn't until I got to know her that I realised she was more reserved than I was. I'd want a cheeky kiss in the pub and hold her hand. If I were with a man doing that, no one is even paying any attention to you at all. But if you're with a woman doing that, there might be a lot more attention than you're maybe used to experiencing. And I think that's what she was conscious of. She didn't want to be seen."

Danni stayed over at Maria's house and was disappointed to find that even in privacy their kissing and cuddling in bed didn't go further. "I was hesitant in my own self, because it was maybe the second time really doing anything with a woman. But I went for it and she was like, 'No, no, no.' And it's like, 'Okay, well if you don't want to then I'm not gonna force you.' It's weird being in a situation when I felt like *the man*. Like, it was very romantic, sure! When I came to our house, we're out on her balcony looking over the stars having a drink. But…"

"When we gon' fuck?"

She laughs, bringing her hands to her face. "Nooo! Not *quite* like that. But I felt like I was taking the lead and she wasn't giving me a bunch of energy. I don't wanna have to be the instigator constantly. I want someone to want me too. Yeah. And I guess maybe the ego plays a bit of involvement.

I'm so used to men wanting that but when it comes to women. It's a little bit more nuanced and it's harder to navigate." She thinks back to Lara. "I never thought I'd be in that position. I now can empathise with how she felt."

I ask about Danni's future, when she thinks of settling down, does she picture a man?

"My attitude's changed. I do think that being with a man is probably 'end game'. I do want a husband. I still sit down every now and again and I think, 'Would I want to be married to a woman?' I think it would be nice. But I do think I want to marry a man. If I had to 'choose' in quotation marks, I'd choose a man. I love women. I think they're so beautiful, such amazing creatures. But it would really take a special woman to make me think, 'Yeah, I want to spend my life with you.' I like who I like. I can find someone attractive, I can want to play with them, I can want to sleep with them, but if I like them? Then that's it; you won't get rid of me. Doesn't matter whether that's a man or a woman really."

As I said at the beginning, Danni is strong. She's a fighter. But much of what she craves from a relationship is to be able to take off that armour. "Outside of the relationship, outside the bedroom, I'm an extremely dominant person. But the only person where I've ever been able to relax into my feminine energy and feeling good in that way…well it's only very recently with a particular guy I've been seeing. He just carries so much boss energy. And it's not like how when I was a submissive teenager with Ryan. This time the dynamics are done right." Despite her cautious optimism, Danni would still describe herself as single. It's early days, and she's been hurt before. "I like the term relationship adjacent," she says pointedly.

"Maybe you could put yourself in the 'it's complicated' category," I suggest. "Okay, I may be showing my age here, but do you remember when Facebook had the relationship status option thing and one of the options was –"

"It's complicated." Danni laughs.

"*Who* was putting that down as their status?!"

"I knew a few people! They'd be like, 'Well it *is* complicated.' And I'd think, 'No it's not.' You just don't want to commit, and the other person does. It's not complicated."

Okay, well, I'm still unclear as to Danni's dating status, but we move on to her sexual identity. Is she a bisexual? Danni doesn't describe herself as openly bi. "If you don't ask, I won't tell you." She shrugs. "If you're comfortable enough to ask me, I will tell you. But I'm still not somebody who's like, 'I'M BI! I AM THIS THING!' You know, it's just not for me. It's in my Caribbean heritage, it's something that's almost taboo. If I had to really, really, really pick, I'd say I'm bisexual with genital preferences. I don't believe that I'm pansexual. The last couple years, I've been so unapologetically me, I am who I am. If you don't like it? Tough."

Danni seems to be in a good place, and I'm happy for her. We come back to her family. If a man is endgame, is that why she's not been open about her bisexuality with her family? Danni's not sure. "Maybe? I think that's a really interesting question. I will never shy away from it. I had an uncle who passed away a few years ago and he had homophobic tendencies – I could see that with him massively. I had another uncle who was gay, who's also passed away, and they got along but they didn't really talk too much. You know? They never really had a discussion about it. But they kind of respected each other's opinions. I was very close to my gay uncle. You know, he knew my bisexuality. He was the only one who knew." She sits back and we're silent. The loud pub antics are a haze around us. I know she misses him terribly. But before I can say anything, she continues on.

"I don't actually think anyone's gonna deny me for my sexuality. And I think it's so redundant nowadays. But obviously, I've got the privilege of living in London and had the privilege of a really open family. I have a trans cousin on my mom's side, my mom's brother was gay. So, if I came up to my mom, I don't think that's gonna be any problem as a bisexual woman. Yeah, there's no real difference. And I just, I'm fine. Like, if someone asked me, fine." And I know that's true. I recall Danni and I in the staff room, a couple of weeks after we met and Danni offhand mentioning a date with a woman. She was recounting not as a coming out moment but as a disastrous date story. They were having a picnic in the park, watching the sunset. They both got drunk, and Danni kept trying to make her excuses to leave. When she finally did, she got lost, stumbling through the park in the dark, and she somehow ran into the date again who stuck around with her all the way to the tube. "I was like, 'It is so dark and I can't see anything – how did you find *me*?!'" I recall laughing and offering some sympathetic comments, but I also recall thinking, 'INTERESTING. SHE'S ONLY TALKED ABOUT DATING MEN UP UNTIL THIS POINT. SO, I GUESS SHE'S TELLING ME SHE'S BI. BETTER KEEP NODDING AND TALKING LIKE NORMAL TO SHOW HOW SUPPORTIVE I AM. **BE NORMAL.**'

I prompt Danni to the memory and she laughs. "It's not the first time. I was talking to a friend once when I was telling her about a dating story and in the middle of it – I swear it was relevant – I said, 'Oh yes! I'm bisexual. Anyway! Bla, bla, bla, rest of the story.' And she goes 'euuuurgh, wait, wait, wait can we pause?' And I said, 'Why should we pause? It's not a big deal!' Anyway, bla, bla, bla, story. And she's just there clutching her chest. Absolutely hilarious. I'm a chaotic energy when I want to be."

We decide to wrap up, go off and have dinner and catch up on the other many things we've missed out on in the last few years of lost connection. I have one more question to go on record. "So, Danni. Does your nan know you're bi?"

Danni's eyes widen. "My one-hundred-and-one-year-old nan?! No; she barely knows my name – that is what happens when you have fifteen kids. And I'm the sixth child my dad had."

"Wait," I say, for the countless time that night. "Wait, what? Then how many cousins do you have?"

A hint of a Jamaican accent starts to peek out. "I don't KNOW, Thomasin. Why would you ask me these questions? You don't want peace! You only want problems! Stop asking me questions you know I don't know the answer to!" She pretends to flip the wonky table and I laugh so hard I wobbles with it. Of all the confessions tonight, this is the most pent-up I've seen Danni. And she's smiling. It's great to see her smile.

And she declares, "This interview is OVER."

CHAPTER 5:
GAY BY CHRISTMAS

"I didn't really see our reunion taking place like this," I say.

Steve smiles warmly and replies, "Me neither."

I'm nervous to see Steve. We were in the same year at drama school together, studying Musical Theatre on a very prestigious course. I think another reason why I denied my bicuriousity for so long was the fact that I was training in a faction so heavily tied with the LGBTQ community. Theatre has been a safe haven for the repressed for so long (for the performers, at least). I was surrounded by some very beautiful, talented people coming to terms with their own sexuality and open to experiences. Surely – surely – if I was down to experiment with girls then the time to do it would have been then, while training in Musical Queerin' Theatre?

"Gay by Christmas," Steve says. "There was that saying." This quote unlocks a flood of memories.

There's another saying I heard once; every dance teacher is a sadist and every dance student is a masochist. For me, it feels very apt. I'm a standup comedian and people applaud me all the time for giving it a go, but they have no idea I've already faced a million heckles from the Head of Dance. I'd be desperately pirouetting, trying to keep up with choreography while making my face look enticing yet playful and he'd be there either yelling outright about my form or – even worse – with his arms folded and muttering a simple, "Horrible." I remember after dance class I went up to him to ask for help with technique and he prodded a specific area on my thighs (it's called the 'saddle bag' by the way – thanks 2000s misogynistic women's magazines!!) and went, "Ugh, get to the gym." I was 5'6 and 54kg. Basically, think Gordon Ramsey as a dance teacher. A comedy crowd full of drunk people who can't tell their saddle bag from their rear end telling me they don't like my jokes or that I'm shit is comparatively not as mentally destructive as people think it is. But an audience full of ballet teachers? Oof. I break out in cold sweats just thinking about it.

I was supposed to be having the time of my life at the age of twenty-one, perhaps even starting to understand my own sexuality and grow out of my teenage insecurities. Instead, I was standing in front of the mirror, hating my legs more than the Head of Dance did. I wasn't great with anyone getting close to my body – girls or boys. And I struggled to open up to people because I couldn't stand the idea of people knowing my business (she says, writing a book for publication).

I was desperately trying to escape from trouble at home at the time and understandably all of my insecurities came out in a lot of my classes. I struggled to fulfil my potential and threw away a lot of opportunities to make a proper career for myself. It had been miraculous that I had gotten into this school in the first place – it was the top Musical Theatre school in the country. I'd only started dancing properly at the age of sixteen and taken up singing around fourteen, yet I'd made it in. Many of my peers had been performing since they were three, but I'd clearly shown potential. I worked my socks off to get there, but it was pretty much for nothing, in the end. It's taken me years to forgive myself for just not having the tools to deal with it all at the time, and as much as my poor mental health got in the way of my learning, the bottom line is I just wasn't good enough. I still struggle to talk to my peers from my degree course from pure shame from the failure of it all. I wasn't unliked, but I had a reputation for being chaotic and insecure, from students and teachers alike. One teacher who I looked up to came up to me drunk at the Christmas party and told me that last year he'd gotten thrown out the party for doing coke in the toilets. "Oh," I say. Then he grades me there and there about our one-to-one singing lessons. "Some weeks you're good and some weeks you're shit." When he sees my face drop, he tries to apologise. I can't stand it. He's out of line but absolutely right. I ignore him and turn around to join a conga line passing by to get away from him. Ever used a conga line as a getaway car? It's slow but sure cheers you up.

While I was mentally imploding, and it felt like my peers were all having wacky and wonderful adventures and #livingthedream! And at the end of it all, dear reader, everybody was right. I wasn't cut out for it. That part of my life would make for a depressing film. The underdog who nobody believes in, who works super hard! Will they make it?! (No, lol.)

So yes, I'm nervous to see Steve.

"Thank you so much for doing this, I'm so excited. What made you want to talk to me?"

"My pleasure," he smiles with a soft Yorkshire accent. "I don't think I see an accurate representation of bisexuals in the media – currently. And I just kind of thought, 'Fuck it. Why not?' I've got no qualms or reservations about it."

When he was younger, Steve was often described as 'ahead of his years'. Now, at the age of thirty, those years are catching up. Steve is of medium height with brown hair and is dressed down in a hoodie; he looks perfectly ordinary at first glance, but he has a warm smile and a grounded presence that you can't help but be drawn to. He sits back comfortably in his seat – his naturally baritone voice booming over the chatter of the pub and clearly into my voice recording app.

Steve's life still revolves around Musical Theatre, where his talents lay. He runs his own adult choir and has been moving up the ranks as a casting director in the industry. Although not on stage himself, he's a respected part of the industry and constantly working. After travelling internationally with his choir, he's now moved back up north and is settling down with his girlfriend.

Steve is an interesting one, he's an open book in many ways that you would expect a musical theatre performer to be, but in other ways the stereotypical northern lad comes out, hardened to cold weather and all other vulnerabilities. He's happy to describe going to a gay sex club in detail but brushes over the fact that he had to change schools due to bullying.

We start at the beginning. Steve had a couple of girl-friends in primary school, all the basics of holding hands in the playground, sitting next to each other on the coaches on school trips and "buying Valentine's card and shit."

"I do have this very vivid memory, I remember walking through Quicksave and it was down a corridor towards the supermarket, and I honestly must have been four or five. And I remember looking up at the wall and there was this HUGE Calvin Klein poster of a model just in Calvin Klein underpants. And I remember being like," he pauses, "I'm not gonna say I was turned on because I was like *four or five*. But I remember being like, 'PHWOAR!'"

Steve first came across the term bisexual at the age of twelve while in his school choir, where they'd sing *Stand by Me*, *Lean on Me* and mash ups of Destiny's Child. Steve loved choir and spent all of his lunch breaks in the music room with his friends, even when sessions weren't happening.

"I was in Year 7, and some teenagers who were maybe in like, Year 9 or Year 10, so a couple of years older. One of them said to me, 'I think you're gay.' And I was like, 'No I don't think I am.' And then the other one said, 'Oh I think you're bi.' And I was like, 'Oh what's that?' And he told me it was when you like guys and girls and it was literally like a lightbulb." He snaps his fingers to indicate the moment, letting out a breath with relief. "'Oh my god yeah, that makes so much sense.' Like I literally remember just being like, 'Fuck yeah, that's like, oh, wow, okay. Yeah. That can be a thing?'"

Steve is not downplaying this memory; it was a concrete realisation and that same year he came out as bisexual to his parents in a heated argument.

"Do you remember what the argument was about?" I ask, my hand on my chest with concern.

"Yeah!" Steve laughs. "Yeah, it was about a boy!"

Steve met a boy called David at an amateur dramatics society he was a part of. "We were doing a show called *The Slipper and The Rose.*"

"Cuuute!" I say vaguely (I've never heard of it).

"It's the story of Cinderella," Steve explains.

"…Why isn't it just called Cinderella?"

The boy at the AmDram was three years older than Steve, which I think is a huge age gap when you consider the mental and physical differences between a twelve-year-old and a fifteen-year-old. "Yes," Steve says, peering down at me with his usual, well-rehearsed line, "But I was very mature."

Danni's words ring in my head. *That's what trauma will do to you.*

Steve can't remember exactly what was happening between him and David, but when it got to the week of the show's performances, David suddenly announced that he had a girlfriend. "I was devastated. Utterly devastated. And so I didn't want to go to school one morning. I'd been so upset, I'd been crying all night. My life was over!"

Steve recalls being stood at the top of the stairs with his parents at the bottom. They're impatient now; if he doesn't leave in the next few minutes he'll miss morning registration. But Steve is adamant he's staying home, armed with this new phrase that he's learnt from the older kids. "They're stood at the bottom saying: 'Why don't you want to go to school, rah, rah, rah,' and I remember shouting down the stairs, 'BECAUSE I'M BISEXUAL' and then storming off into my bedroom."

Steve ended up staying off school that day, and one by one each family member was paraded into his room to tell him that it was okay and that he was loved no matter what. "My gran came round, my auntie came round, I think my granddad was there." The conversation takes on more weight as Steve recalls his father who has passed away. "I don't necessarily believe in fate, but I'm also so glad I had the chance to do that. I had the chance to tell him and he told me, 'I love you no matter what, you know, it makes no difference. You know, whatever! Like, you're young, you know? It might just be a phase, it might be anything, you know. Whatever! But if you are then that's fine.' And I was twelve years old when I came out. Maybe I wasn't ready, and maybe I didn't know. And maybe I've been in and out of the closet ever since then but...I still got the chance to say that to my dad."

Still, Steve doesn't recall being in turmoil about who he was. "They were all like, 'We love you, it's fine.' And I was like, 'Yeah, it is fine.' I wasn't upset because I was bisexual, I was upset because the love of my life had got a girlfriend and he was bisexual! Well obviously now he's not, he's obviously gay—" he stops abruptly, a little shocked at himself and quickly says, "I say 'obviously' because I know now that he's gay, not that it's obvious all bisexuals end up there – but that's terrible still for me to say. But for him the bisexuality *was* a steppingstone; he's gay now. He's living a happy gay life!"

Steve acknowledges his biphobia in the past. "There's a lot of gatekeeping. I've had people come out to me as bisexual and I've said, 'No you're not.' I've been that person. So why should other people believe me when I don't believe it?"

Steve has particularly felt that disregard as an actor in the Musical Theatre industry.

He slept with men, but he told people he was bisexual. "But I think people just assumed I was gay."

When in his mid-twenties and touring the country in a musical, he shared accommodation with two women that he was in the show with. "One of them used to walk around the place we were staying topless. Like in front of me." He says incredulously, "She was so blasé but then I felt like a fraud because I was like, 'She just thinks I'm gay…I mean, would she do this to a straight guy in the cast?! And I enjoyed it. I mean, it turned me on! Because I was like…you know! And I can't tell her because then it looks like *I'm* the creep! Fuck!"

Steve's not been one to date other performers, but he recalls being in another show at a small fringe venue back in his hometown. It was his first show out of drama school and, he was young and foolish. "We were performing the show *Brigadoon*," he says.

"A classic!" I exclaim. I have no idea what *Brigadoon* is.

He grew very close to the backstage manager, someone that Steve happened to have known since he was a teenager.

"I'd told him for years and years and years that he wasn't straight. And he was like no I'm not, no I'm not, no I'm not. He was camp as tits! And I was out and proud, I was like, 'Come on, join me!' But yeah. Then he got a girlfriend."

Although when Steve and Backstage Manager happily reconnected on *Brigadoon*, there was trouble.

Backstage Manager's current girlfriend was also in the cast. The show was only on for a week, but within that time Steve and Backstage Manager started acting on their impulses right under her nose.

"It was really awkward because, even worse, my character's love interest was his girlfriend. So onstage I'm swooning over his girlfriend and then when I'm offstage, we were hidden away necking on with each other. We did get called on it once or twice by people."

"Did anyone tell her?!" I ask, shocked.

"No, no, no, not for like, the week we were doing the show at least."

Backstage of any theatre, there's an intercom – basically a radio in the dressing rooms where you can hear everything that's happening on stage, so you know when to get ready for your appearance.

"I remember that my character dies at the end of Act One. And at the start of Act Two she had this mourning scene over my character. We could hear her crying on the intercom as we were necking on." He grimaces but can't help but laugh at what he once thought was a romantic moment. "It's really bad, isn't it? It's really bad. We were like, proper, proper grinding up against each other and over the radio she's going, 'Nooo, NOOOO!'"

After the show, Backstage Manager confessed to his girlfriend and they broke up.

"And we got together. For about eighteen months," Steve says. "I feel bad but not that bad, I mean it was never going to work out with them, he was gay!"

When it came to dating girls himself, it wasn't so straight forward for Steve.

"At what point do you say it? Because to me it's not an issue. But then if I tell them, say, two months down the line, then they could be like, 'You fucking lied to me for two months.'"

He tells me several stories of dating girls who either ghosted him or broke up with him after finding out he was bisexual. They'd feign other excuses, but later on mutual friends would confirm that Steve's intuition had been true. They'd had a problem "with the whole bi thing."

"It's funny that as a guy seeing when another guy's got a girlfriend and she's bisexual, it's like, oh great! Or like, cool. Well, you wouldn't get that with a girl who has a bisexual boyfriend."

I nod. "It's almost as if it's something to overcome."

"Yeah," he says. There's a long, contemplating pause. "Yeah! And it's always been a big worry. As soon as I meet somebody and start chatting to them and getting close. It's a ticking time bomb. 'When are you going to do it?'"

Steve tells me about having a one-night stand with "some girl at a festival in a tent" while on a break from second year at drama school. They practised safe sex. "It was literally just a one-night stand, but we exchanged numbers randomly. Then she added me on Facebook and then out of the blue she messaged me being like, 'You're bisexual?!' Because obviously at the time I had photos of me with exes or in gay bars and that. I was just like, er, 'yeah.'"

The one-night stand did not send any other messages. "And it's like, how fucking random is that? I think she must have just been confused after looking at my photos. Oh well."

Some women were more intuitive, like Mandy. "I was on holiday a few years ago in Spain with a guy friend of mine. There were two girls that we got chatting to on the first day. We were laying it on thick, flirting and what have you. And we were very good at bouncing off each other. The girl he was interested in turned out to be married, so he was just happy to wingman. So, I remember we were proper joking around, I was doing some kind of skit, some kind of routine, telling them some story. And then Mandy just stopped me and went 'are you bisexual?'"

What a heckle. It's like she had a sixth sense. Can you imagine if they did a whole movie version of *The Sixth Sense* but instead of seeing dead people it was seeing bisexual men?

"Honestly my face just dropped. My friend saw me, and I could see him thinking fuck because he knew my insecurities about it. To me, it was the worst thing she could accuse me of, my arse dropped out, you know? I mean I'm thinking, like this is over. Lost another one. Not again!"

But Mandy was fine with it. It took the pressure off the 'ticking time bomb' and Steve was able to date her without any of that pressure. In fact, Mandy was *more* than keen. "The first time we slept together she was like, 'Tell me what you like doing to guys.' It took me by surprise."

"And what did you respond with?" I ask, ready for some revelling a la Zain.

"No," Steve told her. "'No I don't want to.'"

He inclines in his chair, reflecting. "It had always been two very different situations. So, I like getting fucked by guys, I'm a bottom, I like to be submissive. Whereas with a woman, obviously, I'm not. I mean I can be, but predominantly, it's the opposite. So, when I've got this woman who's like, 'Tell me what you'd like to do with guys,' I'm like, 'No. I'm enjoying this role! I don't want to.'"

While with Mandy, Steve came round to marrying the two sides of himself. "She had this huge obsession with pegging me. She loved the idea of having a threesome with a guy to fuck me. But she also liked the fantasy of seventeen guys on top of her at once."

"Good for her," I declare over my second glass of wine.

"And so actually, I didn't really mind that. I used to suck her dildos pretending I was giving blow jobs to guys. She loved it and I mean – it really turned me on!

"But I'm really fascinated by the fact that I'm like, submissive in one and dominant in the other. Long before I ever had sex with a guy, I used to wank to the thought of being fucked up against a wardrobe. Like from behind, literally up against a wardrobe. And I'd had sex with girls at that point. But I never really got turned on by the thought of fucking a guy. But I guess I am a top and a bottom – it just depends on who the other person is."

Mandy and Steve didn't go the distance, but it had been a positive experience for Steve. Still, he feared it was an anomaly and found himself panicking again when he started dating his current girlfriend.

"We met online. We had our first date three days before lockdown! We met on a Friday, then a Saturday, then lockdown got announced on Monday. So, we did a lot of online dating, Zoom dates, stuff like that. It was really going well. And again, I was like, 'I've got to tell her, I've got to tell her.'"

One night, it comes to a head. Steve has been doing a Zoom meeting with his friends from drama school, doing a quiz night to keep sane during lockdown. They all end up how quiz nights often end up, which is drunk and disagreeing on whether someone deserves half points for a half wrong answer. He tells them about his new girlfriend, how happy he is to have her and how he can't wait to see her in person again. Absolutely trashed, Steve realises that now is the perfect moment to call her up and explain that he's had relationships with men.

"My friends were saying, 'Don't do it. You're fucking wasted, we can barely understand you.'"

But with no one physically in the room to take his phone from him, Steve FaceTimes her. "And she was just like, '...okay, yeah.' I can't really remember what I said."

Waking up the next day, Steve feels an impending sense of doom and calls her back up. He asks her if she really was okay with it. He doesn't want to hear from mutual friends this time. He wants to know the truth.

"She said, 'I won't lie to you, you were so drunk I could barely understand you, but I think I got the gist. And yes, it's fine.' And I was just like," he puts on a meek voice, "'Okay, good.' I don't know how much I did tell her, but I know it's never been an issue. And it's not been as extreme as Mandy, like it's not a kink for her. We don't talk about it a lot – but then we wouldn't talk about ex-girlfriends in detail either. I just have the ability to bring it up. If I want. We've made jokes and stuff."

On paper I appreciate it sounds like he's packed away a part of his sexuality. Once you're with a long-term partner, are you forever only half fulfilled? Maybe it sounds negative to you dear reader, but it's really not like that. From the way he talks about his current partner, it feels serene. It feels content. Call it what you want, Steve is happy.

And his family are happy too. "It's never been a problem with them at all. Like, never ever. But I suspect they're happier now that I've met a woman. My mum, she wants grandkids, I guess. But I think she, as a straight married woman, sees happiness being more free for a straight person. I don't know. Maybe that's not fair of me to put that on her."

It's no secret that for most bisexual people, straight relationships are easier to navigate. But with Steve's social bubble and career being so heavily entrenched with the LGBTQ community, it's been the opposite.

"I'd say it's harder for me. I've almost had to come out as straight. I've had friends I haven't seen since for a while and I'd say, 'Oh I've met a woman' and one of them said, 'Oooh a woman, how modern!' 'Cos they just thought I was gay. I remember I just kept consciously saying to people, 'Oh I've met SOMEONE. I'm seeing SOMEONE.' Rather than say, oh it's a girl. I don't know – maybe I haven't been as open about my bisexuality as I thought 'cos a lot of people thought I was gay. But then a lot of people just put you in that camp."

And now? Does he still identify as bisexual?

Steve speaks carefully. "I think if you asked me now about my sexuality, and not necessarily because I'm in a relationship with a woman…but I think if you asked me my sexuality now, I wouldn't say I was bi. But," he swallows, "it's hard for me to not say that because of my past, and what I've done before. I went through therapy last year, and we dealt a lot with my sexuality. Because it is something that has been a shame and a trauma and erm…a hindrance to me? Well," he says quickly, as if not wanting to draw attention to it, "*formostofmylife.*"

Steve feared going backwards, giving into biphobia or denying a part of his past. His therapist described another scenario to Steve: Think of a man, a straight man. He's been married to his wife for twenty years. Then one day, he comes out as gay and tells his wife. He loves her but he has to leave her. He finds a man and begins dating him. If you ask him his sexuality, he won't tell you, "Well I can't say I'm gay because the past was all with women!" It's about what he's presently identifying and accepting within himself.

"And he said it's the same with me," Steve says, "as I've had a past with men, but that doesn't mean I'm not straight. So yeah. I don't know if I'm even attracted to men anymore."

"And that's okay," I tell him.

Steve shakes his head and smiles warmly at me, in the way I imagine he told his family when he first came out as a melodramatic twelve year old. "Yeah, I know. I know it's okay.

It took me a long time to realise that but yeah." He switches his tone and adds, "But then I walked past a guy today and was like, 'He's fucking beautiful.'"

I laugh. "Sounds like you need another Calvin Klein poster. Or wardrobe."

"I just think it's more sexual. And I think it's more sexual because I'm so insecure about my body. It's a lot harder to have sex with a man than it is with a woman. Because there's that comparison. I had sex with a male dancer once who was beautiful, ripped and had a huge cock."

"Big mistake," I say.

"I was so on edge and ashamed. I couldn't even get an erection, it couldn't happen because I was just like, 'Look at this specimen in my bed!' Like, I was so ashamed."

It's a whole different conversation around bisexuality. Steve and I started out as performers in a pretty tough industry, it's in our nature to compare ourselves to everyone like us; there's always that underlying competitiveness even with the people you want to succeed. But is this something that other bisexuals could relate to? I can't think of anything else in this world that I fancy and want to be at the same time except when I'm looking at a beautiful woman. I wonder, dear reader, if it's something you have thought of yourself? I'm certainly relieved to hear that Steve has felt the same.

'"Do I fancy you or do I want to be you? Do I fancy you because you've got an amazing body or do I fancy you because I want that body?"' Steve believes the therapy he underwent was a big component in helping him understand the difference between the two feelings.

The conversation moves on. We take a breather from the heavy topic of body dysmorphia and discuss drama school (ha!). We relive 'sexy dance'. This is going to sound bonkers[2] but in our second year of drama school, one of our dance challenges was to dance in pairs to this choreographed sort of 'sexy' style dance to an old 80s rock song. Each week we'd do different challenges, Latin dance, 20s dance, that sort of thing. All the students called this one 'sexy dance'. The infamous sexy dance week. At the beginning of the dance, we were told to improvise the first sixteen bars before going into the choreography, and we could wear and do whatever we liked. I had a knee injury that week so I wasn't able to do any of the sexy exercises earlier in the week to prepare us, which included giving our dance partner a lap dance (HELP), and I remember at the time being relieved because as I stated at the start of the chapter, I had trouble connecting with my peers, let alone shaking my sweaty arse in their face. But by the time the performance came around, my body was healing, and with one student falling sick, I

---

[2] Exploitative.

jumped in to dance with a girl called Amber. Wearing fish-nets and lingerie, we shared a clunky kiss as part of our improvised section of the performance, and my only feedback from the teacher was, "You were a good sport to jump in at the last minute." I got off lightly. The teacher paired two boys together who we all suspected were still in the closet (one is out and proud today, one is not). They were highly praised by the teacher for their passionate performance, and I suspect it was intended to encourage them to safely explore that part of themselves. One girl got her boobs grabbed clumsily by her male partner in their improv section. I'm not sure if it was planned with him beforehand but she was determined to show the teacher she could rise to the occasion, grabbing him back and smiling with a stiff jaw. Afterwards when she sat back down with the rest of the class she was visibly shaking. Others got a thrill on how far they could go, stripping and making out in front of people in their class that they fancied. Steve shares his memory of it with a huge grin, proud of his bombastic grinding and biting. Another performer told me how helpful she found it, and how she felt she could take on a role like that on stage in the future after conquering it in class. Others were humiliated. It was supposed to help us get comfortable with portraying ourselves in an adult way. And for some it genuinely helped. Considering how many musicals and dance shows out there sell through sex appeal, it felt like a legitimate part of the curriculum. But it was fucking bizarre, in hindsight, for a girl like me who couldn't even cum at the time. Anyway. Stories for another time. (Buy my upcoming threequel: *Dance, Monkey, Dance: Why choosing to become an actor is the stupidest thing to ever do with your life.* It's gonna be really hard making that one funny.)

Steve discusses our school and the way they'd look at all the young boys in first year, arriving at the school in September, away from home for the first time and dancing their hearts out all day with their like-minded peers.

"'Gay by Christmas.' That was the saying. And I even remember talking to a staff member about it. I mean, yeah, at the time I was well up for it. It was like placing your bets. I was like:

"Him? Definitely. Hell yeah.

"Oh him? Definitely. Gay by Christmas."

Now older, Steve acknowledges that it wasn't such a funny phrase. "What pressure for them! Like, if they heard about it." (And they probably did.) "It wasn't as though we were sat in a circle pointing it out – not that that wouldn't surprise me," he says, rolling his eyes, "I mean we did everything else there."

It was seen as gentle ribbing, but for bisexuals like me, it was a confusing phrase. Not that I was having much sex at the time. Steve's own expectations were high. "When I was moving to London, people told me, 'You are going to shag everything. You are going to shag e-v-e-r-y-thing.' And I was like, 'Yeah I fucking hope so!' But I think I maybe only slept with one person. Maybe." Steve pauses then corrects himself. "Maybe like, four or five, six people? Oh, and I nearly had sex with somebody at college in one of the studios." He chuckles. "It's getting worse the more I'm thinking!"

Steve compares his gay lifestyle to his straight one.

"One thing I miss – well not miss 'cos I'm in a relationship – but one thing I missed in the straight world from the gay world, and it was to just go into a sex sauna and just fuck. I've been to a lot of gay sex clubs. I've never been to a straight one because they're not really a thing."

Steve recalls going to a club with some gay friends.

"Did you have to be naked?" I ask.

"Well, *I* was naked!" He grins. "I remember standing at the bar, having a cigarette and chatting to my mate. And some guy was sucking him off. But we were literally just…we're just having a conversation and some guy comes over. And my friend's going, 'Yeah, yeah. Carry on.'"

Steve pauses. "I think the gay world…well no, the gay sex world can be very intimidating. Especially as a bottom."

Although still a huge ally of the LGBTQ, Steve seems content to leave his own past as a bisexual behind. He's enjoying discovering who he is now, and describes bisexuality as being on a spectrum, more nuanced than the immature 'gay by Christmas' jibes at drama school could have allowed. "Sometimes I could be at a six, other days I'm at a two." But wherever he is, Steve is still Steve.

We wrap up the conversation and wrap up in our coats, heading out into the cold night. We share a big hug at the Hammersmith tube station and then he's gone. I've not kept in touch with anyone from that time in my life, and it's not like the casting directors for a musical will be calling me any time soon. I suspect I won't see Steve again. I don't know it yet but I'm right; he doesn't even respond to the chapter write up that I send him. But it's healing to hear his story, and I hope his happiness continues.

It's strange; when I was younger, I always used to think everyone was having fun except me. I was so obsessed with Musical Theatre that it became my whole life, and I thought anyone who could double pirouette in high heels couldn't possibly be facing trouble in any way. They were all getting better and better, through trial and error the jigsaw puzzle of their adult lives was coming together. Whereas I was trying to play sudoku on a Scrabble board. They were all 'Gay by Christmas' by first year and leaving third year a finished piece, meanwhile I'd spilt coffee all over my own board and was still drying out all the pieces on graduation day. The thing is, I purposely made that gap between 'me' and 'them' so large. It was safer. Maybe it was a way of feeling special, because there was nothing there in my talents to make me feel that way. Not everyone was kind to me, but others were open enough, and now I'm grown I can take better responsibility for the fact that I failed to make connections because I wasn't connected to myself. I wish I'd been able to stop navel gazing so much and recognise people like Steve going on their own journey. I wish I'd made more of mine. God, it feels good to be a grown up. I'm so grateful to have friends now that I cherish. I'm grateful that I found a way to be creative beyond Musical Theatre. And I'm *really* grateful to not need a 'sexy dance' to feel confident sexually. And then I think again about my bicuriousity. It's taken me so fucking long to get here, dear reader. So long to feel comfortable both with myself and sexually with men and to actually reap the rewards. I think somewhere in me I've not wanted to go through those growing pains with women. Like Steve, I have a wonderful partner and I'm more comfortable with myself than before. What relevance is bicuriousity to my identity today? Maybe like Steve, it's something I need to leave in the past.

CHAPTER 6:
AMBIGUSWEETIES

"We were at the top of the tower, keeping watch. Just us two girls. And she reached across and kissed me! I thought, 'Wow!' And that's not all. Earlier on, I'd had a crush on this guy who was bisexual as well, who," Ros interrupts herself, "okay so I'm like, I'm very pure, right? I was raised in a super religiously intense village. Whereas *he* came from a whole other land and my initial reaction was low key *racist*. Right? But then in time it turned to fascination. And then after that, a major fancying of him. And he's very handsome, very muscley, stuff like that. So anyway, fast forward to the day after the tower kiss, we were all up at the top of the tower looking after our friend who had been asleep. The guy I fancy starts working out, and because he's a demon he's super strong. So, he's doing deadlifts, and I'm unfortunately weak, angels are like so physically weak. So, I try to ask him to help me learn how to do a pull up – so he does. But as he lifts me, this guy's hand *slips* and touches my butt! Meanwhile the woman who kissed me is working out next to me all hot and sweaty! So, it's all getting a bit much for my character, these two people she fancies are working out together. She goes to have a lie down and then our friend who we're looking after – who's actually an NPC – suddenly rolls over and accidentally touches her breast! She can't catch a break!"

Ros is talking about their *Dungeons and Dragons* character. Occasionally, she'll tell a whole story nearly entirely in first person, so it sounds like a very bizarre real-life anecdote. There's not much she has in common with her character (an angel who was shielded from the terror of man for all of her life until she met her *D&D* party) except that she is also bisexual. I don't know much about *D&D*, though I find the nature of their stories amusing. I mean, how does a story like that come about? Is there dice involved? Did the character roll a five to touch ass?

"No but that would be amazing," Ros says. "It's more like role play. Like an improv; a collaborative storytelling. Occasionally there's dice, but it depends what you wanna do. If you're interacting with another player, then just role play it."

"So did you kiss that girl in the tower roleplay in real life?"

"Oh, no, no!"

"So, did you narrate it? Like 'And now Storm kissed Galadriel.'"

"Kinda!"

"Was everyone just really horny at *D&D* that day?"

"Oh, always."

I met Ros a couple of years ago at a social gathering, and we bonded over our love of musicals and love/hate relationship with Essex. Once a full-time musician but now working in admin at a music university, Ros is evolving past the hectic life of a London creative. Now in her late thirties, she's moved back home to Essex with her husband, Luke. We meet in central London in Soho, a place that Ros once frequented. Ros, like me, is an Essex Girl. Essex Girls get a bad wrap. They're painted as fake tanned bimbos with thick twangy accents, only caring about material things. Even if that's true, you'll also find they're incredibly witty, strong and fiercely loyal. And besides, Essex girls have to put up with Essex *boys* – so be nice to them; life is hard enough. Saying all this, Ros and I never fit into the stereotype, lookswise, and we paid the price with merciless bullying growing up. We're both pale, soft and bookish, and the famous accent somehow didn't quite stick to us. My accent tends to come out if I'm either angry, really drunk or rather randomly whenever I'm at a bar ordering bubbly, "Shall we ge' some proseccoooo?" Or if I'm around family, of course. Harry says I come home after a visit to my sister sounding like I've had a stroke.

Ros is openly bisexual and proudly part of the LGBTQ community. She won't mind me saying this, but so far of the people I've interviewed, it is the most clear in her outward appearance, and that includes the real life elf prince. Nose ring, purple dungarees and sparkly doc martens, Ros is the picture of queerness. She tucks her short blonde hair, tinged with a wash in pink dye, behind her ears, revealing – and I want to be precise – about eighty-six piercings in her ear.

"Bisexuals are not a monolith – despite the fact that we all wear dungarees and turnup jeans and just *love* the colour purple," she says, gesturing to her own look, "but if we're going to talk stereotypes then of course, all bisexual women are afraid of each other, and bi men don't exist at all. They're just a myth, y'know? Like unicorns. Actually, forget that, no one's bi at all. They're all attention seekers!"

Ros believes that labels are important. To Ros, having the space to label herself proudly offers a sense of belonging, after sticking out for so many years growing up in Essex. Within the LGBTQ community, through friends, online groups and music events for LGBTQ charities, she found the space to own her identity. But it took some time.

"I identified as pansexual for a bit, because I saw the definition and thought, 'Yeah, that's me.' But then I learned that bisexuality was really similar, in fact some people see it as the same. But actually, I just prefer the colours on the flag. Like, I'll fly the pan flag at Pride as well, but there's *purple* in the bi flag!" Ros says dreamily, her face lighting up. I put my head in my hands. Sexuality may not be a choice, but the flag design sure is. "What can I say? It's true." Ros sees the other side of things. "I can see why people would not want labels, I really do. I guess for some people it can be restricting. And also, I have seen so many things online where people say, 'But I'm not sure what I am yet.' And that's fine. It's almost like by giving themselves a label they feel that they can never, ever change? And I see it a lot with the gender spectrum as well. There is, naturally, so much confusion. There are people going, 'What if it's just a phase? What if? What if it's just a trend?' And they're saying that about themselves." She slams her fists on the table with passion, "But Thomasin, *so what if it is*?! That's fine. Where's the rush? You don't have to know exactly what's going on!"

Though from an early age, Ros clearly did. At the dinner table at sixteen, Ros declared her bisexuality to her mum and stepfather. But how did that come about, dear reader?! It took SEVEN YEARS before I saw my sister hold her boyfriend's hand in front of the family at a formal Sunday luncheon. How do some families talk so openly?! Ros thanks her stepdad. "He just comes up with the most random stuff. Like we'll be chatting over dinner and he'll turn to me like, 'Have you ever done weed?' Not even in a way to ask if I'd been smoking weed, just sort of, out of interest."

I narrow my eyes. "What's his angle?"

"I don't know!"

"Maybe it's just a typical stepdad who doesn't know how to communicate with his teenage stepdaughter."

"I think he likes to be hip. So that's where that comes from. 'I'm cool and down with the kids, I'm gonna ask about their sexuality!' He's a cool guy. I mean with the weed thing he used to grow loads of it!" (That *is* down with the kids.) "But yeah, I think I remember saying to my mom that I was basically as likely to bring home a girl as I would a boy. Which is completely inaccurate because girls are terrifying." She laughs, shaking her head. "So terrifying."

I get it, actually. Like Ros, I faced bullying from people I found attractive. I was a chubby pale geek with an aspiring monobrow who liked anime, but when I turned eighteen, I suddenly became Essex Girl hot. I danced all week in preparation for a budding potential in a Musical Theatre career, so I got super fit suddenly. I dyed my hair blonde, I waxed my arms, I tanned and tanned and tanned. Suddenly I looked like all the other girls, and it was great! And the boys? Well, they changed their fucking tune. From kicking my chair to calling me hot, it was a really jarring experience. Suddenly I'm feeling power over boys, I'm feeling attention from them, and I *like* talking to them now – it's easy to talk to them, THEY SEEM SO INTERESTED IN WHAT I HAVE TO SAY! It took me years to realise that I wasn't talking but *flirting*. I had about twenty guy friends and I would go clubbing on Wednesday nights in Chelmsford, get my jaeger bombs bought for me and would grind up against most of them in appreciation as I danced. It's embarrassing now but it felt like pure fun at the time. My first boyfriend wasn't exactly pleased about the attention though, so I stopped waxing, stopped tanning and said goodbye to Grinding Wednesdays. I eventually felt like more of a human woman than a potential love interest to my guy friends, but I still entered my twenties with a chip on my shoulder about trusting girls. Even now, as a proper grown up, I sometimes find that little weirdo in me scared to talk to girls in case I make a fool of myself, platonic or romantic. And I want to make it clear that this is not me being like, 'I'm not like other girls' because I *absolutely* am. The problem is entirely my own insecurity, dear reader. And the fact that I have the capability to fancy a woman makes the whole thing even harder. I mean, the *audacity* of my sexuality:

My brain: I can't make friends with girls :(

My sexuality: But maybe you could sleep with them :)

"I know!" Ros says. "It's terrifying. I don't have a gaydar either. After busking once I was having a chat with someone and we were talking about feminism and I was saying, 'Yeah I'm a feminist' and they went, 'Yeah, obviously.' I mean, 'Okayyyyy?!'" She laughs. "I mean they were a feminist as well; it was fine. But I don't get how people can tell this stuff. I didn't get how they knew."

"Were you singing a song like, 'I hate men! I hate men!'"

"That's my entire set list."

Back to the dinner table and a sixteen-year-old Ros, Ros' mother was pretty non-responsive. "Not in a kind of judgmental way. Just, 'Oh, okay. Not for me, but fair enough.' I don't think it was ever a secret."

"Was it the dungarees?"

"It's probably the amount I used to watch *Moulin Rouge*. And – oh, yeah," they say this enthusiastically, as if the memory just popped up, "*so many* awakening music videos from the noughties. Like Britney Spears, Christina Aguilera. Or t.A.T.u!"

Oh god. I'm younger than Ros but I remember t.A.T.u – vaguely. They had a song called 'All the Things She Said' and the music video was of two girls dressed in school uniform kissing in the rain. I remember how fascinated and uncomfortable the video made me – I was terrified of being caught watching it and accused of being a lesbian. But watching Nicole Kidman writhing around in *Moulin Rouge* was a pass. Hey – it's Academy Award winning! I AM ALLOWED to be watching this, right? But t.A.T.u? It was too much. I couldn't pretend why I wanted to watch it, so I didn't.

After comparing notes on noughties music videos, we get back to Ros' childhood. Did she have crushes on boys growing up?

"Oh, EVERYONE. I kind of felt like bisexuality is sexualised in a way that, like, we're all constantly horny and wanting threesomes?"

cough Zain cough

"Well, that's not true of every bisexual obviously. But I was kind of, like, always thinking about *romantic* things. I'd fantasise about stuff from a young age. Like, literally every person I came into contact with, I'd be like, 'I'm gonna marry that person.' I was in Year 2 at school when I asked out my first ever boyfriend and I think," she looks up to the ceiling, counting, "*two hours* is generous. It lasted two hours. I looked him up recently. He used to look like a pea with a face, just a perfectly round head." She sighs wistfully, as if talking about the one that got away. "He looks exactly the same."

When she was aged ten and at a sleepover, Ros had a realisation. "Nothing weird happened. But I remember looking at a girl thinking, 'I like her in the way I like boys. I'm romanticising her in the way I would boys.'"

It wasn't an alien concept to little Ros; her father was a long-running member of their local amateur dramatics society. "It's probably why my dad wouldn't blink an eyelid at my sexuality. Loads of people in the group were bi or gay. I was around them a lot from the age of three, so I had a lot of gay influences – oh my god!" She interrupts herself, yet again, as a memory comes to her. "Like the first time I ever saw a penis!"

One day, as a child, she and her father went round to his best friend's house to drop something off. "This best friend who was also in the theatre group was gay."

At his house, little Ros notices his computer desktop background. In the present, adult Ros puts her hands under her chin as she remembers, her mouth open in shock. She kind of looks like that famous painting 'The Scream' by Edvard Munch. Little Ros walks closer to the computer, squinting her eyes. "And it was…" She stops and collects herself. "So, you know when you're with a group of friends and someone takes a picture from below and you're all putting your heads in the middle, looking down at the camera?"

"Yeah," I say.

"Yeeeeah, it was like that but with penises. My dad saw too and was like, 'Oh my god.' We went on his computer and found a very small picture of his friend dressed as a Dame in last year's panto and made it like a tiled background instead. So, it went from HUGE dicks to the most off-putting sexual image we could find." She shakes her head, reliving it and quietly muttering. "Massive, massive penises."

I ask, "Are you sure they were huge or were they just huge in comparison to your size as a kid?"

"I...in my mind it's a crystal-clear image. And they're like...Thomasin, they're like a torch!"

Ros first dabbled with their bisexuality as a young teenager, around the age of fourteen with a tomboyish girl friend called Ange. "We used to go out to these rock nights at a community club on Fridays with our friends. And yeah, one time we ended up kissing. It was a pretty cool moment." But despite an obvious attraction to one another, they never went further. Ros sits back in her chair, not saying for the first time about someone. "She was the one that got away, I suppose. But in reality, it never would have worked, we were so young and so different. She was too anxious to travel to London, whereas I was thinking of one day living in New York! I didn't want to live in Chelmsford much longer than I needed to."

Once they finished their GCSEs, Ange and Ros lost contact, but reconnected in more recent years when a good friend of Ros' connected with Ange on a dating app, which blossomed into a serious relationship.

"When she found out I'd married a man she said to my friends, 'But Ros is gay.' She couldn't recognise that I was bi. It really sucked. It was stupid."

Ros talks about another sleepover (did all of her personal growth happen at sleepovers? All I did was eat sweets in my sleeping bag). "One of the most amazing experiences of my entire life when I was about fifteen or sixteen was with two of my friends the same age. One of them was definitely bi, the other one, maybe bicurious but like, I kind of felt like it was an entirely gratuitous event for me. We had three-way make out sessions. And we were all wearing silk nighties like some kind of made-up fantasy."

"So how does that even happen," I ask, perplexed. "'Hey, you know what would be really random? If we…'"

Ros honestly doesn't remember. "Maybe they planned it between them?! I think maybe we joked about it, because we've kind of committed to the silk robe kind of vibe."

"Are you telling me you bantered so hard it actually happened?"

"I'm a liberal flirter. I would flirt with them, I would refer to kink all the time. So, there was a lot of flirting. I used to flirt with my bi friend all the time. We used to sometimes go around her house at lunchtime – this sounds so weird – but we would go there and do the dirty dancing moves, but to like noughties music, you know?"

I put my drink down. "Wait, sorry, just so I'm clear. In the middle of a school day, on your lunch break, you would go back to her house, and just dirty dance together?"

Ros grits her teeth into an awkward smile, as if she's in trouble. "Yeaaaah."

"When you say 'dirty dancing' I'm thinking of *Dirty Dancing* with Patrick Swayze with the ballroom moves. Or do you mean you were," I think of Christina Aguilera's

Dirrty music video, another terrifying experience for a young Thomasin, "*dirty* dancing?"

Ros flaps their hands dismissively and says, "No, no, that would be *crazy*. Just like the Patrick Swayze ballroom moves. And then we'd go back to school."

I look at her.

"She lives so close to school," Ros says.

"Yeah, the logistics aren't what I'm questioning here."

"Why, was that weird?"

Ros also had a friend called Loz who she adored. Loz would tease Ros, telling her she thought she might be bi but she wasn't sure, but never in a way that Ros could take seriously. "I liked her so much. We'd go out, she'd get drunk, and then we would make out and it was very nice. And I was fine with it, I don't think either of us really necessarily wanted any kind of commitment from each other. But I told her at one point that I was in love with her, which wasn't an uncommon declaration for me."

"*Did* you love her?"

Ros sits back, sucking her teeth. "Probably not. I think I used to be quite obsessed with love as a kind of concept. I'd probably watched *Moulin Rouge* that day."

Ros has always been intense with her romantic relationships, steering wildly from one crush to another. It took until her marriage now, where she and her husband have agreed on an ethically non-monogamous relationship that she's learned to take her romantic ideals with a pinch of salt. It's a new term for me, and I find myself tripping over the term as it comes up again and again in our chat.

Ethical monogomous

Ethically mon-nomogonous

Ethnically non-monoogonous

"Ethically non-monogamous," Ros says, the phrase rolling off her tongue easily. In short, dear reader, it means that Ros and their husband can have romantic relationships outside of their marriage. It's different to polyamory, in which someone has multiple partners; Ros isn't planning to marry or move in with anyone else, her husband is number one, and their mutual respect and love of each other is supposedly what makes this work – but more on that later.

As we walk around Soho to find another bar, I reminisce about my experience here. I remember visiting London with my boyfriend at the age of eighteen before I moved officially to the city for drama school. We did all the tourist trap stuff. "Look!" my boyfriend would say, pointing at the views from the London Eye. "Look!" my boyfriend said to nearly every wonky wax figure we saw at Madame Tussauds. "Look!" my boyfriend cried, pointing at the M&M store, where we emerged an hour later with nothing because we were eighteen and poor and M&M alarm clocks are fucking expensive. We found ourselves wandering around Soho. I remember seeing two men walking in front of me suddenly hold hands.

"Look!" my boyfriend said again, pointing like it was another attraction.

"Shut up!" I hissed.

"What?!"

"Shh!"

But it wasn't his fault. We'd grown up in Essex in the early noughties, it was just as astonishing to see two men openly hold hands without fear as it was to see a waxwork of Hitler. (Why did Madame Tussauds have that?!)

I tell Ros about when I first moved to London and my initial hope for Soho to be some kind of cool, gay hangout for me as a student. But I was immediately priced out and only now in my late twenties am I able to come out every once in a while and bask in the queerness. I still haven't been to Freedom.

Alongside her list of recreations, Ros is an occasional Drag King and Drag Queen, though they have found they much prefer the latter. "I was telling a friend about how much more comfortable I felt being very overtly sexual as my Drag Queen. And she said if I can only do that if I feel like I'm being perceived as a *man* dressing up as a woman, then surely that's anti-feminist."

"That's a hot take," I say.

"Yeah. It was fucked up," Ros says. We walk in silence for a few moments "It's an interesting discussion though, because there is misogyny even in the gay community. Girls as Drag Queens, gay men have told me to stay off their turf. When the first kind of white cis woman on *Ru Paul's Drag Race* was announced, this person was saying to me, 'I just don't understand why they didn't give it to someone who was LGBT.' But Thomasin, the contestant was literally a lesbian. But people forget, like…" She stops, and I can see she's trying her best not to generalise, or vent too hard. She speaks again, a little guarded, a little quieter. "It can really feel sometimes like the cis male gay community forgets that there are other people. They are not the LGBTQ plus community as a whole. There is an L. And then there's a B."

"I mean I can't believe we have only *one* lesbian bar in Soho," I say, finding my own gripes coming to the surface. "That – guess what? Isn't that great."

"There's always a massive queue for the ladies," Ros declares in solidarity.

"That's actually what the Q stands for in LGBTQ. That's what that is. That's how long it is." Despite my complaints, I do love going to the ladies' toilets. Everyone always asks why women spend so much time in the ladies' toilets on nights out, but any woman knows it's because it's fun! You can make friends over the hand dryer! You can have a little sit down when your heels are hurting! It's feminine, it's safe and the lighting for selfies is great. In that sense, a lesbian club is like one massive ladies' toilet.

"When was the last time you went to a lesbian bar?" I ask Ros.

"Two weeks ago, but all I picked up was a cold."

Instead of the lesbian bar, we settle on a cosy pub, sharing the cheapest bottle of red wine that we find. Ros tells me about the last time she came to Soho. She met up with a girl. Was it a date? Ros wasn't sure.

"I thought that it could be a date orrrr I could have made a really nice friend. It's impossible!" Ros puts her head in her hands before drumming the table with her fingers. "I got *two thirds* of the way before I realised that it was not a date." She looks down at her hands and realises they've become disgustingly sticky after drumming on the table and exclaims, "Oh."

Our cheap wine arrives and we clink glasses and cheers. "It tastes slightly like Ribena," Ros says, "but not in a way I can't get behind."

We go back to this date. Ros had met this person at a music event and had had mutual friends. She was an artist and Ros was convinced of LGBTQ themes in her work. "I'd text her. I said, 'Hey sorry if this is out of the blue but do you wanna go for a drink sometime?' Which I think is pretty forward! And she was like, 'Yeah sounds good, where and when?' And I was like 'OH DAMN IT'S HAPPENING.'"

After lots of hair swishing and flirting, the 'date' mentioned her boyfriend and, when Ros brought up her ethical non-monogamy with her husband, also noted that she was monogamous. "For me it's double complicated. It's not just about bisexuality but it's also being like, 'No really, my husband's cool with it.' I want to ask people what their situation is and explain my situation, but you want to put it across in a way that isn't predatory, you know?"

We talk about Ros' husband. He's forty and works in events, often travelling to the US and working around the clock. Together for fifteen years (and married for five of them), Ros first met Luke at university, flirting over a tarot card reading.

"I was reading a lot of tarot at the time. I read for him and then read some for myself in front of him." Ros reenacts the scene, she pulls out a card like a burlesque dancer pulling off a glove, pouting her lips. "Oooooh!"

I've got to admit, it kind of works.

"This one card came out when I was doing his readings. And it was the star card, which is basically a naked woman leaning over a pond, pouring water into it from jugs. She has her jugs out and she has her jugs out, right? So, the way I do the whole tarot thing is I think of the traditional meanings of the card, but I'll also look at what stands out in that moment. And it can be quite different from the person depending on the reading. That one I was, like, very aware of boobs."

Ros finds herself unable to do her usual reading, getting flustered. She looks Luke square in the face and points at the card as she says, "Tits."

And that was that.

This is Ros and Luke's first marriage and first ethically non-monogamous relationship. Right after they married, Luke was called away on another event in the US.

"It was really challenging, partly because stuff happened at my old job. My first relationship was abusive, and a colleague came in and they had an abusive relationship. They weren't recognising it. And that triggered me, it was tough. And Luke was away."

At the time, Ros was listening to a podcast called *Pagan Friends*, the guests that week were two sex workers and porn artists who were in a lesbian relationship together, but also ethically non-monogamous.

"And the way they put it made it sound like common sense. 'Yeah, I love her. Why wouldn't I want her to have a lovely time? I know one person can't completely fulfil another person.' And I thought it made so much sense. And it kind of relieves the pressure a little, you know? There's this idea of like, you know, one person being your everything and in reality, it's not really like that, is it? And yeah, if you're kind of interested in more than one gender, then it's a whole other thing. My husband is also bi, by the way. Though it's taken him a while to come to terms with it."

What happened next? Nothing for a long time. Then a couple of conversations. Then more nothing. Luke had been reading this book which also questioned the concept of monogamy and had been having similar thoughts to Ros.

"You were both on the same page?" I ask.

"Yeah – both of us thought that it was our idea! So, we're both thinking, 'I don't want them to agree to it just to make me happy.' Another friend of Luke's was approaching non-monogamy herself. She was reading about it, joining groups on Facebook, and she was going to meetup brunches. We went to one with her and her husband. I was wearing my finest dungarees and more purple lipstick, which apparently made me *very* popular.

"So, she was exploring it and I was almost tagging along for the ride. With Luke and I, it was in the air. But I did notice that he was getting close to someone at work. A guy. And I just thought...wouldn't that be CUTE?! It felt like some kind of slow burn romance. One night, when he was back for a week, I turned to him in bed and said, 'Do you think it could ever get sexy with him?' And he said, *'What?'* And he had to take a minute to be like, 'Wait, you would be okay with that?' And I thought, 'Yeah. Yeah, I think that would be cool. Like, I want to see how it goes for you. You seem to be making a connection that's more than friendship, so I don't want to stop you from exploring that.'"

Of course, it's always easier to say things than follow through with action (that's why dirty talk is so powerful). As soon as Ros waved him off to the airport for an overseas event project, her stomach dropped and panic set in. "I went on this crazy rollercoaster of emotion, mainly abandonment issues. Then I thought, 'No, we're making this decision. If he didn't want to be with me, he wouldn't be with me.' We'd also talked about a successful marriage." Ros leans forward, swirling the wine around their glass. "I don't consider a successful marriage one that lasts forever. I consider it to be one where you can love each other enough to see when it's not right. I think that's just as successful. And for us, this is still very much right."

With this in mind, I find the way Ros put her fears aside for the sake of Luke's exploration commendable. Ros shrugs. "Well, I figure it's a get out of jail free card! If he goes first, then I can do what I want!"

Unlike Steve, despite also being with a long-term partner, her bisexuality is still hugely relevant now that she is ethically non-monogamous.

"I have a friend who came to terms with her bisexuality later on in her life and found it really difficult to talk to her then husband about it. She was just kind of like, 'I guess this is just it forever.'" Ros shakes their head. "And that's SHIT. That's shit for you, and it's shit for your husband. It's shit for you because you can't be yourself. There's so much that society puts on you in terms of things like monogamy."

Still, things aren't always plain sailing. Ros tells me about a friend called Natalie, they were old uni friends, but hadn't been especially close, more showing up at the same sort of parties together. Ros found out with surprise that Natalie was in the same situation – she and her girlfriend were giving an open relationship a go.

"I don't think it was quite official at the time. Her girlfriend wasn't ready to settle down and wanted to go for it."

Still, Ros and Natalie decided to go on a date. "I was bothered by not putting a label on it. She called it 'ambigusweeties.'"

"That's a weird phrase," I say.

"Yeah," Ros says. "Yeah! And I like to know where I stand with people. So, it took me quite a while to be like, 'What do you mean by that?' Apparently, it's more than friends but not a girlfriend. Which I get; there's a scale of friends that I would fuck. There is one end saying 'friend I would fuck' and the other end it's 'friend I would not fuck.' I kind of feel like ambigusweeties is somewhere beyond 'friend I want to fuck.' I guess it's like an intimacy thing where you can be like, emotionally intimate. And also, you know, sexually intimate – but not expect anything from each other, I guess? But for me that was jarring."

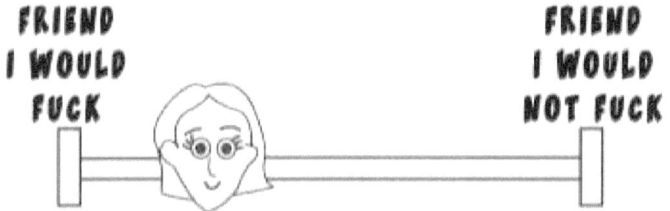

FRIEND I WOULD FUCK — FRIEND I WOULD NOT FUCK

Up until this date, Ros' sexual experience with women was, "A lot of making out and what you could vaguely classify as fingering." It was nerve-racking.

Their first date consisted of going to a life drawing class. "We had fun, but I didn't realise how awkward life drawing is. But then first dates *are* awkward – might as well lean into it." They shared their first kiss on a bench. "I don't know why but I always have my first kiss with people on a bench. I think it's a proximity thing – I sometimes don't know how to interact with people on a human level, I don't know how to initiate things, so a bench is fine because you're already sitting next to each other, you're already super close. The bench does half the work! That's a hot tip for any bisexuals out there." Ros leans into my recording device like it's a dating tip and says, "Go on a bench with someone you like. The odds are something will happen. The closer you are in public, the better the odds." Ros launches into a projecting voice as if doing a Ted Talk or advert, "Kiss on a bench, finger on the tube, eat out on the bus. Ladies: it works!"

And work it did; Ros and Natalie went home together. They had dinner and drinks and watched *Moulin Rouge* and didn't touch the whole evening. Ros stayed in the gues-troom, but Natalie climbed into the bed with her. Ros shakes her head, trying to recollect the whirlwind that hap-pened next. "And then as soon as the light went out, it was like, like, just, you know, *making out* and it was really fast as well! I kind of went with it for a bit, I think she was definitely nervous. For context as well, it was the first time her partner was away with someone else. So that was playing on her mind."

Ros felt uncomfortable with the speed and took charge, focusing the energy on Natalie. "I was okay with doing stuff to her. I just didn't necessarily feel like there was enough leading up to it for *me* to kind of be in that headspace for sex. She seemed to have a nice time, then we went to sleep." In hindsight, Ros really didn't like the 'ambigusweeties' vibe, and she and Natalie – without discussing it – simply stopped meeting up. "I had been really keen to define it, that's what I know. Because as cool as I am with people still figuring out their sexuality, telling me you're confused is still a better answer than no answer, y'know? And you want to know what the fuck is going on. But she's got a lot of stuff going on in that house, or maybe she's just not interested. It's a different situation with my husband – I'm not having to be non-monogamous to make the relationship *work*."

Dating men outside of their marriage hasn't been a smooth ride either. "There was this one guy who I'd been sexting, like sending voice notes during masturbation – which

160

is hot, by the way." After a few months of this, Ros cycled to his place.

"The sexiest method of travel," I say.

"Oh I was so sweaty when I got there! I'd just got the bike so I was very excited about it. Free travel and trick exercise, no matter the occasion."

Ros hangs out at his flat, playing darts and flirting.

"I have a darts stance that's very sexy," Ros brags.

"What, bent over with your leg up?"

Ros talks him into letting her cook them a vegetarian dinner, which turns out to be the wildest part of the night.

"He asked at one point, 'Do I have any weird things about my body?' I said 'Not really...I don't think so.'"

I snort. "What a weird question."

Ros presses her lips together and puts her hands together. "Well."

"What?!"

"He had one testicle. And I felt like he was waiting for me to bring up, 'Oh you only have one ball. How interesting.' I'd seen them in the naked selfies he'd sent. I think he wanted a reaction, but I wanted to be cool about it! I'm sitting there thinking, 'Well it would be rude to bring it up!' So, we ended up having sex without either of us talking about it. It was a bit awkward."

Needless to say, their lack of communication failed to launch their sexting into anything more meaningful. It's still a hard concept to get my head around, being ethically non-monogamous. But as Ros says, it has given them and Luke that freedom to explore parts of their sexuality that the other can't fulfil.

"I feel like it's been more of a significant step for him in terms of exploring his bisexuality. But I think that regardless of bisexuality, it has strengthened us. Like, I feel like in order to successfully be ethically non-monogamous, you have to be very secure in the relationship. And your communication. And your ability to communicate needs to be strong." I don't feel like I'm a possessive partner, but it's difficult to imagine me not throwing plates if my boyfriend Harry was to sleep with another woman – or worse, fall apart and have my heart absolutely B-R-E-A-K. But for other bisexuals in committed relationships, I can see how it could work.

I find myself confiding in Ros in a way I haven't yet with my interviewees. "I feel like if I was *really* bi, something would have happened by now."

Ros shakes her head. "But it's so much easier to be in a straight-passing relationship. That's the path society leads you down from the get-go. The next morning when saying goodbye to Natalie at the tube station, we had a little kiss, and then I immediately thought, 'Oh shit, am I gonna get hate crimed?!'"

"I feel like I've been cowardly," I say.

"I don't think it's any reflection on you. I mean I'm married to a man! And it's because of representation. We see a man and woman interact all the fucking time on TV and that. So, we can learn how to interact with men through them. We learn the game and the coding. And then as women you're taught to be vaguely nice to each other. And then after that it's really confusing. For my husband's bisexual experience, I think he's found it a lot easier. He's found it easier to hook up with other men, but not necessarily connect emotionally. Whereas I'm a whole hot mess of crushes on people that are not going to go anywhere!"

"I feel like I'm a strong ally," I say, defeated.

"Noooo, you're a *part* of this community."

"But I don't always feel like I am," I say. I think of how amazing it felt for Ros to find her identity after being bullied back in Essex. I think of how amazing that feels for me too

– but is it genuine or am I just trying to find a sense of belonging somewhere? Am I blowing these feelings way out of proportion? (I mean, if I'm writing a whole book about it after getting a crush on a girl who plays a Drag King, then yes, probably.)

As sure as she is in her bisexuality, Ros relates the feelings of my confusion to their experience of gender identity. "That's how I felt when I heard the term non-binary. Some people get body dysmorphia due to it, or don't want to be referred to as a man or woman. I didn't feel any of that anguish or feel anything that extreme, so I felt as a fraud as telling people I was on this sort of non-binary spectrum. But I kind of realised that there are increments. And the more I was just not judging myself, the more I could realise that I wasn't necessarily cis. The more I was kind of like, okay, so maybe I want to try she/they pronouns. And then, I don't know, the more I kind of relaxed into it, the more I was like, oh, no, this is actually like, this has been a long time coming. I just couldn't see it."

For Ros, it was through talking to other bisexuals that she discovered the term demi girl. "I always thought I was a cis woman, but at times where I felt at my lowest, I felt like I didn't have a gender at all – but that was like a very self-esteem-based thing. Demi girls kind of identified as like, maybe 80% female and 20% non-binary. I always thought that non-binary equals androgyny, but being non-binary doesn't mean that you can't be fem or masc. It was really interesting. I felt like I'd almost had the wrong name tag all this time with being a cis woman. A couple of months ago I would have said I was a demi girl or demi woman. But now I feel much more comfortable with genderqueer." She shakes her head, "It's such a weird thing to try and define yourself, even if it's just in your mind to yourself, but I want everyone to have a lot more patience than themselves and just be like, 'Okay, I like this right now, I feel like this right now.' And it's okay. If you change your mind, that's just life!"

For Ros, the way they've been able to connect most to their femininity is as a Drag Queen. "The amount of times I used to say, 'I'm not a proper girl, I don't know how to do hair and walk in heels' and how uncomfortable I would feel presenting as super feminine. I do think that partly is a self-esteem thing. And I don't want to be defining a woman's experience by saying how I don't feel those things – it isn't accurate. Every woman experiences their identity as a woman differently." She thinks back to her early experiences, seeing her father doing pantomime in their local am dram. "I always wanted to be the Dame. And I remember having a little phase of being jealous of the fact that men could grow facial hair. It's no surprise to me that the way I want to display my femininity is in the stagiest way possible. Ru Paul is on record as saying for women to be in drag, there's no danger there, there's no risk. He compared it to women having Miss World. But Miss World isn't for every woman, and I don't see it as empowering. And guess what – it's dangerous to be a woman *every day*."

Miss World certainly never felt for me. It didn't feel like a dangerous thing for a woman to be a part of unless she fucked up by being caught with drugs or tweeting something silly and getting kicked out of the whole thing. I don't mean this as any offence towards any woman who enjoys those competitions or even Queen of Drag our holy Ru Paul, but you don't transform yourself in those competitions the way that a man does to Drag. You conform.

"Miss World is about being desirable," I say.

Ros nods. "And presenting as being desirable doesn't necessarily present as being sexual. It feels dangerous to be slutty, mouthy and outrageous and outrageously feminine in a female body. And Miss World is archaic. There's a gender performance that is ripe for parody."

So, what's next for Ros? She has her eyes set on a new conquest. "Someone who I went to university with who I'd had a crush on for so long, I thought she was clearly not a cis woman and not straight but she maintained that she was. She was due to marry a man then Covid happened. During that time, she broke up with him. I've seen her twice at friend reunions and she's not said anything about the breakup to me. I talked about being a demi girl and she said, 'Oh that sounds like me.' We didn't talk sexuality though. She was really tiptoeing around that. But I've heard she's now a bisexual from my lesbian friend! And I'm not gonna bring it up to her like 'I know,' but then we had a hen do we went on recently and she flirted and teased me *relentlessly* the *whole* time!" Ros talks faster, excited. It's like she's talking about her *Dungeons and Dragons* character again, but this time the scenario is real. "And she knew I was ethically non-monogamous. So much of flirting is power play and she was *deliberately* making me blush, looking me dead in the eyes. We both went back to our own homes and were texting each other, and she was making suggestions about me dating women. And it was hard 'cos she hadn't come out directly to me, but I mean C'MON! You're being so obvious! But I was like, 'The ball is in your court babe!' I don't know how clear I can be without telling her directly. But maybe I won't have to," she says slyly, twirling her glass of wine. It's like a villain revealing their master plan. Ros grins, "maybe she'll read your book and send a text my way."

Wait.

Wait!!

...is my book a wingman?

CHAPTER 7:
CHARMING

"Any decent musician has either sucked cock or at least *thought* about sucking cock."

Andrew gets right into it. He is a *dirty* man (in the Christina Aguilera sense), and I don't think he'd mind me saying it. We meet in a busyish beer garden and sit at a table in the corner. The ground underneath us is slanted so we're at an odd angle and just like with Danni, the table wobbles when we gesticulate too much. But no loud group of lads. It's a quiet area where we can talk privately.

It's 12 pm. I order a cup of tea, my first one after rolling out of bed ten minutes before I left the house. Andrew goes for a beer.

A talented pianist, Andrew and my boyfriend Harry go way back. They first met as precocious kids at a Saturday school that helps nurture young musicians, and they later attended a boarding school for talented classical musicians.

"I hate classical music now." He sneers, and it doesn't feel like hyperbole. He really means it. "The industry is brutal

and elitist, so now I do anything else. As long as I can play."
And he does, from teaching kids to playing in bars to musi-
cal theatre shows abroad (though that last part is harder since
Brexit). He's even supported a well-known pop act on tour.
Andrew is a rare being – a full-time musician.

We start where you'd imagine this story starts: at boarding school. Boarding school sounds both magical and hor-
rific to me; when do you find the space to masturbate? I picture the *Harry Potter* dormitories with ten beds in a tower
surrounded by the large, judging eyes of cats and owls and
talking portraits.

"It wasn't quite like that," my own Harry tells me. "You
shared a room with just one other boy. You could do anything you wanted really."

"And did you?"

"We'd joke about stuff like, 'Alright well you go for the
shower first 'cos I need my morning wank.' Or he'd say, 'Oh
don't look in the dustbin 'cos there's a wet hankie.' But I
think Andrew *wanted* me to look in the dustbin."

Harry and Andrew shared a room for a while, but Harry
was kicked out and forced to move into another dormitory.
"We weren't good for each other. We got up to mischief –
not sexually. More like stealing plant pots from around the
building and then moving them all into one tiny classroom."

They'd had a warning, but Harry still finds Andrew one
day in their room with a black bin bag he's filled with water.
Their dorm is the highest part of the building and before

Harry can ask what he's doing, Andrew lobs the bin bag out the window and into the teacher's car park.

"It landed with such a splat that I was crying with laughter. What I didn't know was Andrew did a runner as soon as it landed. So, I'm there with my eyes closed, I've fallen off the bed I'm laughing so much, I'm holding my sides. Then I open my eyes and I swear Andrew has disappeared and there are three teachers looking down at me instead. I was in A LOT of trouble and had to move rooms but Andrew somehow got away with it. He could be very charming."

I wouldn't necessarily call Andrew charming. What he is, is handsome. Very handsome. He's thirty, tall and with jet black hair and brown eyes. Combine that with excellent musicianship and you've got a heartbreaker on your hands. Andrew is not an arsehole by any stretch (is there a dirty joke in there somewhere?) but he isn't on the charm offensive. In fact, he speaks his mind rather brashly at times in our interview; he has little care for whether I like him or not.

"Arrogant," Harry says matter-of-factly. "He could never take notes."

Andrew is more than happy to admit his fallout at school. "I'm not that interested in that sort of crowd nowadays. I'm not even friends with anyone from that world – besides Harry, though we haven't talked in years until he messaged me about your book. I felt like I could never live up to expectations or the bitchiness, so I was just like 'alright fuck you, I'll do something else.' I'm not a bad player of course but some of these producers – the ones that get me out on tours – they can't tell the difference either way. They're always wanting me because they hear I'm," he puts on a snooty voice, "*classically* trained.' Or how I like to say, 'trained.'"

Andrew grew up in a lower middle-class household, and he got into boarding school on a partial scholarship and "dead grandmas' inheritance." Full of anecdotes, he shares a similar sense of humour to Harry – as well as his Scottish accent. Though Andrew's Glaswegian twang is a lot stronger. If I had the knack for it, I'd probably be writing out his speech in the way Scottish people spell out their words, all *dinnae* and *cannae*, but I think you'd agree that an English person doing that would be downright ghastly (heavens *me*!). So just watch an episode of *Still Game* or something and just imagine that in your head for this chapter, okay?

I remind Andrew of the pranks he pulled with Harry and he sniggers. "Those days made boarding school actually bearable."

Despite both men experimenting later on in their lives, Harry and Andrew were never aware of each other's bicuriousity at the time. Before me now, Andrew seems to practically show off about his escapades, and for the first few minutes I think I have another Zain on my hands. But the more we go on, the more I see that uncertain teenager who was closed off from himself. Andrew is surprisingly vulnerable.

"I guess there's this common trope of people who go to boarding school, that they've all experimented in their dorms together. But that's something I never did. Not at boarding school." But he wanted to. "My peers would tell me all the stories and then I'd go and have a quiet wank in the corner."

Andrew recalls a time with his new roommate, Frank. "We were kind of – just out of interest – looking at some porn on my laptop. It was straight porn. But this kid in our year barged into the room and caught us. Nothing was happening but later he told me he was delighted and secretly hoping we were jerking each other off."

Wait. "Do guys watch porn together?" I ask, confounded.

"I dunno, yes?" Andrew shrugs.

I try to connect the dots, thinking of my own experiences. "I suppose it's a bit like how girls go to watch a *Magic Mike* show together. It's kinda like that?"

"No, I think it's very different 'cos girls probably don't finger each other during a *Magic Mike* show."

"Is that what guys are doing when they're watching porn together?!"

"This really sounds like an interview," he replies sarcastically.

"Thank you – are you gonna be giving me notes as we go on?" I retort.

Andrew burps in response.

Charming.

173

I actually have been to a *Magic Mike* show – you know they have a stage show in London now? It's basically just dancing, stripping men. I went as part of a hen do and was disappointed to find it wasn't a musical with a storyline. The whole thing was too intense for me, dear reader. Call me old fashioned but I just feel like I need to know a guy's personality before I can comfortably peer upon his penis – not that there was much of that to see from our cheap seats. I found myself feeling very awkward and making little asides every time a guy would come hip thrusting onto the stage like I was reviewing the show, "He's got a really commanding stage presence." In the end I just leaned into the whole affair and drank an entire bottle of prosecco to myself. It was a rough night in the end. I threw up in my purse.

Andrew was raised in Glasgow in a loosely Catholic household. Although never discussing his bisexuality, in hindsight, Andrew realises his parents had their suspicions.

"I remember once when I was talking to my mum about my schedule for something – I was maybe twenty – and I said I don't care about the agenda, as in I don't mind what the plan is and she fell about laughing, incredulous and said, 'Oh my god I thought for a second you said I don't care about gender – oh my god – I was just thinking that's the last thing I need!' She was laughing *so much*." He pauses. "At the same time my dad used to randomly say things like if, 'If you were gay, we'd still love you and it would be absolutely fine.'"

Andrew describes himself as an effeminate child growing up, and some of his friends that he'd bring home from boarding school were gay. One day at the bus stop before he's due to go back to school, a teenage Andrew turns to say goodbye to his mother. She suddenly blurts out a question.

You're not gay, are you?

"The implication behind the question was, 'You're not one of these lesser humans, are you?' Like, there was concern there. I said no. It wasn't followed up with anything reassuring like, 'Fine and if you are that's alright.' I think my dad was always nicer about that stuff, even though he was the one who'd make vulgar, silly jokes. Like 'Oh don't drop the soap if you're in that place' or 'You're gonna need a lot of kitchen oil' or whatever."

"Sorry, WHAT were you and your dad talking about? Those sound like tips to me."

"Oh, I don't know, my dad is very vulgar. He says some silly things but he's very non-judgemental. I'm sort of the same."

Andrew's recalls his first crush at age three. "There was a girl I went to playgroup with. She was going around in a little white dress and I thought, 'She's cute!' I also did have a crush on my primary school teacher. She was pretty. And you don't know anything about anything at that point. You know naked bodies are covered up and you think it's funny. Everyone learns at some point about sensation. I'd stumbled across badly labelled VHS tapes in the house. They didn't say spread legged ladies or anything, but they'd recorded something off the cable TV. I think I was about seven. I remember watching that and seeing all these naked people doing stuff at the gym. Naked girls doing star jumps and gymnastics and stuff. British porn is so softcore, they're not allowed to show anything penetrating, not an erect penis or even a penis really. So broadcast TV porn is different to the internet where everything is..." He blows a raspberry, making a squelching noise.

Jeez. In the age of everything being at our fingertips, it's sometimes difficult to remember how we used to live not too long ago. When people talk about life before technology, I think of bus schedules and trying to find a pub without Google maps, but I can't believe people used to have to plan the logistics of when they'd *tape their porn*.

The Catholic guilt in Andrew was very real. Andrew's grandpa was a minister, pious and very much dead by the time Andrew hit his teen years. "It took me years before I gave in to play with myself at all. I thought hmm, he might be watching. I didn't know if all these people were still ghosts and watching me! Then one day I thought screw it, no one's probably watching. I remember getting pleasure, my stomach tensing and I thought okay that's probably what sex feels like. It was erect and then it stopped – now I realise because I'd climaxed. But I thought I'd broken it! I very nearly went to my dad like, 'My dick's broke, what do I do?'"

Andrew's instincts were to fantasise about women sexually, but also romantically. "Even when you're a kid you can see why males and females want to kiss. And I could identify with that. But the first thought that crossed my mind that I could be something other than straight was when I was recalling some of the porn I'd watched and thought hm, 'I wonder if it feels good for the guy there.' I remember getting a bit hard and thinking, 'huh. Bit weird.'

"Once in the changing rooms at school, all the showers are open. Everyone looks around, even if they're straight, they're just body checking like teenagers do, comparing sizes and that. But I remember once or twice I was talking to myself in my head, begging myself not to get hard. But it was also kind of exciting too."

"Have you ever had romantic feelings for a guy?" I ask.

177

Andrew goes quiet. He looks down at the bench he's straddling. It wobbles a bit.

"This is a very poor design," he says. "I can smell weed."

"I can smell weed," I agree.

The beer garden is still peaceful. We can hear someone mowing the grass in the distance, and the occasional car whizzing past the main road. Andrew has stalled.

"Let's talk about your experience with girls," I suggest. "When was your first girlfriend?"

Although his boarding school was mixed genders, students were strictly forbidden from staying in each other's rooms at night ("not that it stopped us.") When he was sixteen, Andrew managed to bag an eighteen-year-old girlfriend. An age gap like that in your teen years is practically ten years as an adult, but after an arrested development Andrew was confident. "The woman has to be okay with the concept, and then I'm very assured sexually. If a girl's like 'come fuck me' then I'm like 'FUCK YEAH.' But before then, we'd be making out and she'd say, 'Ooh I'm getting horny' and I thought, 'Well that's a nice thing to know.' I didn't know about these things! I thought I had to wait weeks and weeks and then I'd get to pet something. I didn't think I was allowed!"

"I snuck into her room one night. She came out the shower smelling like coconut. She took her towel off and lay on the bed and I dove right in with my tongue. And she came in like two minutes and was *very* happy. And that was my first sexual experience." His first love ended just before Andrew went away to university; she cheated on Andrew, so Andrew cheated on her. He moved to London with a full scholarship to a great music school, single, free and away from fear of judgement from his parents. But he was still terrified of his bicuriousity, so, just like at school, he didn't confide in anyone at university about it. (I really hope people can forgive themselves for not doing all the soul-searching exploration and crazy parties that people expect you to do. It's difficult enough to get into uni and then take on that financial hardship to worry about whether you're *finding yourself*.)

Andrew was more scared of the emotions tied to the physical act of being with a man. "I didn't want to hurt someone's feelings or mess around with someone. I didn't want anyone to call back or be involved in my life at all." He was exasperated: "I just wanted to play with some *dick*. So, when I turned nineteen, I just marched into a gay sauna. It was a very extreme and weird sort of place – for me at the time anyway. Now, I just humour most of it."

Covered only in a towel, Andrew walked down some "dark corridors" with hands of much older men coming out to touch him. It sounds like a carnival haunted house experience.

"There was this one drunk, deranged guy sitting on a chair near the pool just going 'Waaahey' at every person under fifty who passed by. It was weird and seedy. Then I saw a guy in the corner, he flashed his penis at me so I was like, 'Oh right I'll do it the same.'"

"Like flashing your lights at another driver?"

"Look, at gay saunas eye contact is enough to be like, 'Please destroy my arsehole.'"

Andrew and this stranger go into a private room. The intrigue changes swiftly to nerves. "I didn't know what to do. I didn't want to kiss the guy! I just wanted some penis."

The stranger quickly realises it's Andrew's first experience, so he offers him the chance to top.

Which was very polite of him, I suppose.

"I put on a condom and tried but he was too tight he just said this ain't gonna work. 'You're cute, be careful. And for god's sake, you're way too young to get the worst stuff, use protection always.'"

Strong advice that stayed with Andrew, but his Catholic guilt warped it into a condemnation.

"The next day I was in class and it suddenly hit me. The worst thing ever. What if I've contracted something? What if I've got HIV? Of course, I hadn't, what it was was guilt over the seediness of exploring it. A part of me felt it was unacceptable to be doing anything with a guy, to be doing that opposed to something," he puts his fingers into air quotes, "*normal*. And it turned to terror for three months where I genuinely thought maybe I'll die of HIV soon. I played *a lot* of music."

For the next three years he was too scared to even approach a man. It also affected the way he approached girls.

"I thought I can't be with a girl because she won't want to be with me if I have something. Or it would feel like a stain on my integrity for the rest of my life. At school all they would do was go on about the dangers of STIs. They don't realise the ramifications of avoiding all the good reasons for people wanting to have sex. It's about pleasure and enjoying each other's bodies. It's not a transaction."

I think back to my own sex-ucation (can we make that a new word? I feel like it's a good word). We got taught the basic biology of course. One of my biology textbooks had a page of a man and woman tangled together, naked but see through so we could see how it was working on the inside. I'd inherited my text book from someone in the year above me and he (because it was obviously a he) had scribbled above the drawing an encouraging,

GET IN THERE MY SON!

We had maybe one teacher in the whole school who was willing to talk frankly, and he had a reputation among my peers because he was the first person to introduce us, aged about fifteen at this point, to the fact that you could buy flavoured condoms. He definitely taught us more than that, but that was the biggest takeaway.

"There's chocolate flavour...raspberry flavour...banana flavour..."

BANANA?! We'd all shriek.

The education was a bit inconsistent though. I remember my older sister coming home from school and telling me how they all had to put condoms on a banana for practice and she proudly told me that she'd applied hers so quickly that the boys in her class had remarked on it, impressed. *Oh great,* I thought, *another opportunity for me to look like a fool in front of my peers. Not only am I a monobrowed, chubby geek, the boys are going to find out whether I'm going to be good at sex. Come to think of it,* I'm *going to find out if I'm going to be good at it.*

But the day never came, the closest we got to bananas in my class was the mention of said flavoured condom. I sat there all term thinking every lesson, 'Maybe today is banana day' and was always left disappointed. Honestly, I was sitting there so stressed about heterosexual learnings that I don't think I had enough headspace at the time to properly consider any kind of queer side to me and how the hell that worked. To this day, I still don't really know how to put a condom on a guy. I give up halfway and sit back, frustrated, horny and craving a banana.

Despite a clean STI check, Andrew couldn't think straight. "I just thought of these sauna guys, they were all dirty and seedy and full of disease to me. It was like an evil seediness that was in my head. But I still had all these urges." It didn't take long for Andrew to dip his toes back in, and today he's a true convert, gladly diving into a sea of penises. He tells me a few of these stories, including one about (consensually) tying a police officer to his bed that is way too graphic for me to put in this book – much to Andrew's disappointment. "It's so *easy*. It's so easy to dial-a-dick. It could be between fifty to a hundred people who have sucked me off now. Grindr is great for that. The profiles without a picture and without names are usually the straight ones writing."

Andrew met his next serious girlfriend Rachel at an open mic night in London. She was a couple of years younger and also an aspiring musician, shy, sweet and in awe of Andrew's musical skills. "Rachel was very innocent and, I don't want to say spoiled, but she had a very *nice* upbringing in Putney, and she stayed at home for the whole of her uni degree. By the time I got with her I knew for sure I was into guys, but I didn't think it was something to approach with her. She was just very sheltered." At age of twenty-three, Andrew went over to the US on an exciting project, and they went long distance.

"Something happened when I went away. I think Rachel just went wild, discovering her independence a bit when she moved out of her family home."

Andrew found himself saddled with another cheating girlfriend. "It was the most intense time of my music life, I was recording this album and it was going badly. I was being treated horribly and questioning the whole music industry. It was the middle of the day, in the thick of it. Rachel called me on the phone and said, 'I've just taken my cheating to a new level; I just sucked this guy off even though I said I wouldn't. Sorry.'"

Fucking hell. Ethically non-monogamous this is not.

"I said, 'Let's not even begin on my reaction to that in itself, but this is the worst time you could have even told me that, why could you not have just waited until another four hours when I was done with work, why?! I've got to go back in there and *work*. She said, "Cos I felt guilty I needed it off my chest.' That's so selfish. It's not well-meaning, it was all about her. 'I needed to tell you, so I told you.'"

Hurt, humiliated and half crazed with jet lag, Andrew fires back with his own hidden ammo. "I said, 'Oh well yeah big deal Rachel, I've sucked cock too.'" He then goes on in great detail to explain his dial-a-dick lifestyle before he met her. "I just didn't care anymore what the backlash would be. When we first met, I was still at a point where I wasn't sure if girls would be weirded out or whatever. We were together for like, four years. The whole time she never knew, I'd never given any indication either. She was suddenly acting all furious like I was just as bad as cheating. Like, 'How the fuck could you not tell me, what the fuck? I'm not mad that you're bisexual I'm just mad that you're not honest da da-da da-da.' Then she started crying, 'You're just saying that 'cos *I* sucked someone else's cock!'"

After breaking up with Rachel, Andrew had a wild ride touring the world and hooking up with men and women. He met a girl called Gemma. "She was then a complete change from Rachel. Gemma told me the first night I stayed at hers, 'I was a bit slutty in my early years. I contracted anal herpes, here's some pills if you want it.' Anyhoo! We had a good time, we were safe. But I'd hooked up with a guy three weeks before that. Gemma didn't know I was sort of bi…ish. This guy I hooked up with," Andrew sucks in his breath, clasping his hands together and lowers his tone, as if on trial, "I'm always careful. Oral sex is fine, but I know stuff can be transmitted. Always use a condom for anything penetrative. That was one of the rare occasions I got fucked. And

I thought I noticed something on the end of his dick, I thought maybe it was a bit of fluff. I said, 'What's that?' And he said, 'Ah, nothing.' He put a condom on…but he'd used his fingers on me already."

Shit.

"I did an STI test after Gemma as we both agreed to get checked out." A few days later, while watching a concert, Andrew's phone pings loudly. People tut around him, Andrew is embarrassed and annoyed with himself for not putting it on silent. *This better be good.* He pulls it out to do so and sees the text on his homepage: YOU HAVE ANAL GONORRHOEA.

"I'd been fucking Gemma unprotected that weekend, I'd just been pulling out." He cringes. "Anyway, I told her. It had not made its way to her thankfully, it was localised in my…there," he says bashfully. "It hadn't made it to my dick, so her test was negative. But she went absolutely ballistic. She said: 'I don't mind you liking guys and stuff but I had no idea you'd be *hooking up* with guys, that's fucking disgusting, it's so dangerous.'"

It was the first time Andrew faced such vitriol. He shrugs. "What could I say? I put her at risk. Though this was someone who had contracted STIs by getting fucked raw herself – so it was a bit hypocritical. And then a few months later when I ended things, that's when she *really* blew up, calling me dirty and all this shit for being with guys. Every nasty description under the sun that she could find she said to me."

Now in his late twenties, Andrew decided to take it as a lesson. "It made me realise never again would I hold off being perfectly comfortable and open about bisexual stuff with any potential female partner. From the outset I will mention it as if it's as normal as the weather. If it's an issue for them, it's much better to lose that potential girl than to take on that headache."

Although he's honest with his women, it's still not a conversation he's having with his family.

"I wouldn't say I'm out and I wouldn't say I'm in the closet. It's quote on quote 'not that fussed.' It's not such a big thing for me to make a big deal of like, I'm not going to make my Pride post on social media. It happens in such private circumstances that it doesn't need any more attention, especially to my family. There's always that fear that maybe if I made something bigger of it then it would change the perspective of me or what people think of me. But I talk to some of my friends about it and they don't really care. That being said, I wouldn't talk about my love of dick like I do my love of pussy as I don't have that romance with guys like I do with girls."

He nods at me. And that's that. So that's Andrew's story, dear reader. All's well that ends well!

But that's not entirely true, is it Andrew?

CHAPTER 8:
BUT WAIT! THERE'S MORE

Andrew met Seb when he was fifteen. He'd just won a prestigious piano competition.

"The previous year's winner shows up to give the prize, like they transfer it. This guy was a year and a half older than me. He was American, mixed race and a very tall and pretty boy. I always thought Seb was pretty. Some people say he thinks he's the smartest person in the room a bit too much. He uses his pretty face a lot to get what he wants. But I liked him. We lost touch, but when I went over to the US around the time I was having trouble with Rachel and having that shit time at the job I was on, we reconnected."

Andrew and Seb talked a lot online and, when they were in each other's countries, would play together.

Andrew slows down, playing with his empty beer glass. "He met the love of his life in Seattle. They were a couple since they were, like, twenty-one. And they live together in California. Everyone thought of them as the cute glory couple. They'd travel around together, post lots of pictures."

"Like a power couple?"

"Not a power couple but a cute couple. I'd go and stay with them a bunch for concerts and stuff. Or just for holiday. I"—he's stammering now—"I *played at their wedding.* I put as much into it as I could. I made people cry. *I* even cried a little. I never cry." It sounds nice but Andrew's saying it in that cold, careful way that people do when they're preluding to trouble ahead. I look at Andrew quizzingly and he shrinks in his seat. He says again, "I always thought Seb was pretty."

Andrew was finishing on a music tour in Chicago and Seb came to watch. The plan was then to make a road trip from there to New Orleans where Seb's husband was at the time, on a family visit.

"We did lots of fun things. Seb had always done so much for me, helping me get work, giving me a place to stay, showing me America. He'd been really great. We make an overnight stop; I can't even remember where. But we're at this house, sitting in the living space with this amazing view out the back. I'd been gifted all this booze from this job I'd done so I'd just brought it in the car, and we had a great time. And *I'd always found Seb pretty.* I'd always liked those lips. I almost wanted the comfort of cuddling another guy at one point," Andrew frowns, the feeling still alien to him now. "I don't know. He was getting cuddly and I was getting cuddly, on this couch. I just wanted to feel elbows and arms. Something actually just intimate, and affectionate – for once. I'd been away on this job and it had been fun, but I'd felt so lonely too. Being there with Seb felt so *comforting*. Like something I'd missed or hadn't done."

But Seb realises it's getting too intimate. He giggles, pushing Andrew back over to the other side of the sofa. Andrew, also drunk, rolls over and falls asleep wordlessly. Andrew's heart is racing. He stares at the ceiling.

We're just friends. We're just drunk. We're just lonely.

It's a close call, in many ways. Something nearly happened. Maybe Seb is Andrew's one that got away. But instead of starting drama they did what most people approaching their thirties start to find joy in; they go to sleep instead. Phew. So that's that. All's well that ends well.

It's a pity that it's another lie.

CHAPTER 9:
A HELPING HAND

"Aaaargh I don't know if I can do this!" Andrew says, back in the present.

"Keep pushing," I say like a midwife.

They did fall asleep. They were drunk. But something in Seb cracked.

"I woke up and the sexual tension in the air was…" Andrew trails off. "Before I know it, he's on top of me. And we're kissing passionately like crazy. He's grabbing me, he's almost catatonic with it. He hadn't touched anyone else in ten years."

"Except his husband," I say quietly.

"Yeah," he mutters, shaking his head, disgusted with himself. "*Married.* I was friends with them. I'd stayed with them. But it was…" he sucks his teeth, "All the clothes came off. We're doing all those things. I was inspecting his package, as I'd been told that it hmmnuunmen." At this stage the guilt has physically incapacitated him. He buries his head into his hands, right down to the table. It wobbles and I steady my cold half full cup of tea.

"Sorry?" I say.

"His dick was a nice size," he says from behind his fingers.

"Okayyyy," I sing breezily, hoping my chill vibe can somehow counteract his melancholy.

"I mean not like colossal but a good – he was a tall guy – I'm not a dick judge. Sorry I'm going off topic here."

Could that be a job? Dick judge?

Dizzy with booze and fuelled with years of unrelenting desire, Andrew tries immediately sitting down on Seb. It hurts. "I said, 'Shit you're gonna need more than spit on it.' That sort of brought him to his senses. And thank god because if he'd slipped in we'd have fucked until he came – but we didn't do that. Which is good."

Seb and Andrew stop and look at each other. *What are we doing?* They move apart and try to laugh it off.

Dick Judge

"Bad idea."

After silently nursing individual hangovers, they set back off on their road trip.

"As soon as we got in the car together, we spoke like normal. After hours and hours of talking about other stuff he just suddenly smiled at me and said, 'You're a bad influence.'"

Andrew has since kept his distance from Seb and his husband. He misses them, but he's trying to do the right thing. Let me remind you that all people make mistakes, dear reader. Straight, religious people cheat so much that God told them to stop doing it in the Ten Commandments. Like, if that's in the top ten of priorities then it's got to be rampant. But that's not the point of this story.

Andrew continues, "The point is that after that, days after that I couldn't stop dreaming about it. I just wanted to do it more. Even if it wasn't sex, I wanted to just kiss him and be intimate with him in the way you would with a girl. We talked in the car, and he just laughed the whole thing off like, 'Ahhh, guess that can't happen again and guess we can't tell anyone we know, right?!' And I told him, 'Yeah of course!' But I had all these new feelings, I guess feelings of affection for once...And that was different. I was really enjoying it. He said he was glad to have helped me with that – but that lesson is OVER. And not to be discussed again. Sadly, if it had been an opportunity, I would have jumped on it. Even though it's terrible, with him being married. So that's the whole story. It's bad isn't it? Evil. I felt terrible. And alarmed. There was an *alarming* level of passion ignited with Seb."

It was a curveball after years of animalistic sex with no feelings getting caught. "There'd been twing, twang, pangs of feelings like that before but since then I have thought, 'Ohhhh, could I have had a boyfriend? Or have I missed that type of thing? Is it something I would have wanted or liked? I never quite found all the satisfaction I wanted from sex with men. I never got what I wanted, which was the genuine, normal, circumstances under which some curious guys might experiment and take it from there. Like how it was in the beginning with girls, with Emily. I always felt so removed and fractured from that because I was scared to be seen to be acting on that. And what if I did and it freaked me out? What about the emotional attachment that I would get?" Andrew then steers in a completely different direction and states proudly, "I've done everything sexually that I can with a guy. Oh, except get fucked by a guy while I fuck a girl. *That* I haven't done."

"That's a lot of stuff if that's the one thing you haven't done."

Andrew scratches the back of his head, grimacing. "I think maybe I need to be more honest with myself about the internalised biphobia growing up. I mean the whole Catholic thing didn't help. And I think it has affected how I treat sex with men as opposed to sex with women. I love seducing a woman, and I love being wanted by her. I love just cuddling with a girl sometimes, it doesn't have to be sexual. Whereas with a guy, I wouldn't be one to seduce anyone. Anything I did had to be very clear. There was zero cuddling or kissing because that would be fucking disgusting to me – or to girls like Gemma – as opposed to all the dirty stuff we'd get up to. That's really what I thought for a long time. It grossed me out. Guy-on-guy stuff grossed me out. But man, it made me cum so much. I thought being bi made me messed up."

But when did that change? Andrew credits his platonic friendships with gay men. "Spending so much time with gay people who were living normal and fulfilled lives and had communities with each other with full support and acceptance. It did help. I never thought growing up that gay people were 'worse' or 'less' like some people growing up in homophobic environments can think, but I thought *I* would be if I was that. It stopped me doing anything experiential that I should have done for the sheer terror of if people knew they'd laugh about it. If only I'd had a tenth of the social competence that I have now."

"And it's not a lot," I say jokingly, trying to lighten the mood. "So, do you think that if you'd had the confidence you had now back when you were even fourteen, do you think it's possible you could have had a serious boyfriend by now?"

Andrew fidgets in his seat. "Possibly. Maybe. But I love girls too much and I wouldn't have wanted to have closed myself off to that for any length of time. But I'm also not closed off in the way I used to be."

In a similar trajectory, I also feel like Andrew's less closed off than the start of the interview. We decide to wrap it up, but just before we part ways we go back to the start, revisiting Andrew's boarding school experience. So many teenagers experimented. Were they all bicurious? Bisexual? Or were they, in fact, straight?

"Oh yeah, the majority of them. Like I said, a lot of guys would watch porn together but just wank side by side, I think there's a sense of camaraderie in that. There was no anal sex swings."

"Even with private funding? Shameful."

"I mean, isn't that the premise of your book? 'What is bi?' But also, what is 'straight'? Surely if someone's straight they're gonna at least be able to get off with their friend jerking them in front of heterosexual porn. I don't know if there is or isn't any bicuriousity there. It's simply, they're comfortable with their friend, they've seen their friend naked, they've maybe even seen them fuck some girl or something so what's the difference? It's a hand that helps. Helping hand, they call it," he says sagely. "But then again it was a high proportion of musicians who probably do subscribe to my philosophy in life which is, may I remind you, 'anyone good at music has either sucked dick or thought about sucking dick.'"

There you go. All's well that ends well.

CHAPTER 10:
THE RELATIONSHIP
THERAPIST

"I have one story," Veronica says.

Okay, so, I have to start by saying I am ninety nine percent sure that this lady has more than one story, but she only has an hour to spare on her visit to London, so she settles on her biggest one.

Veronica is the sweetest person I've interviewed, but boy does she get herself into trouble. She's that fateful combination of incredibly trusting and incredibly beautiful. She's curvy and has the exact same lips as Angelina Jolie; they're the first things that stand out when I find her on social media. I've cheated a bit with finding Veronica – I didn't actually know her before this interview.

"If you're interviewing me," Andrew said, "then you've got to talk to my mate Veronica. You'll love her, she's gorgeous." I do. And she is. I'm convinced she's photoshopped her face to hell on her Instagram profile but not so. It's great to see her in person; she's a great impressionist. I don't tell her this as I don't want to make her self-conscious, but she's very fun to watch, expressive and full of different tones and accents.

Veronica's father is British, but her mother is French Canadian. She grew up mostly in Vancouver before coming to the UK for university, but she sounds more like a Californian valley girl, complete with a heavy vocal fry ("I like, totally licked her out"). She's lived adventurously, travelling the world through a cruise ship job for most of her adult life, but now approaching forty, happily married and with a five-year-old and three-year-old to keep her busy, Veronica's settled in the UK. She lives just outside of Manchester and trains puppies learning to be guide dogs (it takes all of my focus to not derail the precious time we have into puppy talk). We sit down at a charming coffee shop called Fuckoffee (complete with paper takeaway bags labelled 'Shite') by London Bridge and she takes me back to a time when she was at her most trusting: nineteen and travelling alone for the first time.

"I would frequently go to Quebec, mostly to see my extended family but I'd love just hanging out on my own. I would go there for half term and just wander around. Quebec has a lot of tourists, and I don't have too many friends there so a lot of the time I'd be going to my favourite pubs to drink and think about my ex. But I'd also meet people, usually tourists and sometimes I'd meet people from the UK which was awesome 'cos we could bond over something mutual. There was this one evening where I was down this Maple Wine Cellar. Each floor you go down in the pub, it gets more grungy. Like on the first level it's like a beautiful wine bar and then you go under and people start smoking cigarettes and beers are served as well. You go down another level and then you might smell marijuana and you maybe start doing shots. You go down a level and it's like, really cheap drinks and like, people are doing coke in the bathroom and other drugs, stuff like that. But the ground level is beautiful."

"That bar is like Dante's *Inferno*," I say.

"That's exactly how I've described it before. Like I think I've used that exact reference, it really does feel like you're descending into like, total sin and hell. Each level is open later. Once one is closed you just go down. They tease you with the fancy wine then before you know it you're doing coke in the bathroom."

While on a half term break from her second year at uni, Veronica was travelling without her mother for the first time. After a day spent visiting her grandparents and collecting some belated birthday money, she found herself about to enjoy a night's descent into total sin and hell at the Maple Wine Cellar. At the ground level wine bar, she notices a man and a woman trying to order a drink. The man is leaning over the bar, asking about something specific but struggling to communicate with the waiter whose English is limited.

Veronica walks over casually and translates. The man and woman look her up and down as she takes control of the situation and Veronica feels like a grown up. She turns and smiles at the couple and they smile back.

"We developed a friendship from there. They were giving off major, *major* sex vibes from the beginning. I remember thinking, 'Wow these guys are reaaaaally horny,'" she drawls, accentuating her vocal fry. "The girl was maybe eighteen and she was a dancer at the Royal Academy of Dance in London. Her partner was this, like, this thirty-eight-year-old, maybe pushing forty."

Uh oh.

Veronica notices my face change. "Mmhmm. Yeah. But he was a *relationship therapist.* And he'd written books, so I guess he was legit?"

Well, yes we all know if you've written a book then you're legit.........hi :)

"I wish I could remember his name 'cos he wrote this book where he used this circus analogy when it comes to relationships. You ask a person – this is how he roped me in," she pauses, putting a hand to her forehead in shock as if the reality of her sharing this story is just hitting her. "This story is so crazy for me. I haven't had an experience since or before." She shakes her head then continues.

"So, the analogy was like, you ask somebody with or without their partner, you tell them to close your eyes and imagine you're at the circus. He goes through this whole script that he walks through where he really gently takes you through the smells and the sounds and what's around you and the excitement of performing and what that would be like, and finally, what would you *be*. What would be your act? What would you *do?* I think that I said to him I wanted to be like a gymnast on an elephant, like, going around the stadium but on top of an elephant. And if I remember correctly, I think he gave me some kind of," she says, trailing off before then affecting an impossibly deep macho voice, it kind of sounds like Vin Diesel. "'Oh so this means you really wanna take risks but you need like a solid MAYN underneath you to support you and make you feel safe,' like some bullshit like this. But at the time I was like"—she changes her voice to a fluttery, high pitched Kardashian squeal— "'Wow you're so wise. I can't believe you can tell me about myself!'"

Veronica was only a year older than the girl with Relationship Therapist. Truthfully Veronica can't remember her name, but knows she was training to be a ballerina. "Ballerina was really beautiful, so delicate but poised. We were chatting and drinking and very quickly it was clear that there was something, some kind of energy. It wasn't just chemistry. It wasn't normal. I had an attraction to both of them and they're obviously together, and I didn't feel guilty 'cos I felt equally attracted to the two of them. So, it was just like a perfect sort of dynamic. But anyway, they left – they left

Quebec – and they added me into a WhatsApp group. It was called, like, 'We 3' or something like this."

It was the three of them, Ballerina, Relationship Therapist and Veronica. They started chatting a lot and very quickly intentions were made clear. "He was really the initiator. She was just kind of there like 'yaaaay' and 'yes!' and ' 😊 '. And she also seemed very comfortable and calm with it all, very confident in her body…it sounds awful, but she really came across older than eighteen. Though she was quite petite like a ballerina, right? Like short, shorter than me. And very slim. Much slimmer than me. And he was Greek, he was quite hairy." She snorts, I think out of embarrassment rather than amusement. "I wasn't physically attracted to him, but the charisma was there with him, and the physical attraction was there with her. Does that make sense? So anyway, they made it very clear they wanted to have a three-some," she says matter-of-factly, flicking back her hair and it becomes clear to me that this is only the beginning of this tale.

But wait, how did we even get here? Let's go back to the beginning.

F
 L
  A
   S
    H
     B
      A
       C
       K

Veronica's experience with girls started young, having a huge crush on Pamela Anderson as a child.

"There was this famous photo when she's wearing these suspenders," she says excitedly, "with like, leather. And they're covering her nipples – it's this famous photo. I used to print them out and put them under my pillow. Pamela Anderson and Leonardo DiCaprio equally for me, I don't know why."

I nod my head and immediately Google 'Pamela Anderson leather suspenders' on my phone under the table. Though there's no need to hide it; Veronica is doing the same thing.

Veronica laughs as we scroll through our phones. "Oh my god I was obsessed with her boobies." She sighs wistfully and then frowns at her phone. "Oh, I can't find the photo. I can't find any photos!"

I'm distracted. "I mean I'm seeing *a lot* of photos. A lot of photos of Pamela Anderson right now."

Veronica grew up with both parents. Her father was twenty-four years older than her mother, but despite being an older father Veronica always felt close to him. "The topic of sex was spoken about through a good sense of humour – 'cos my dad had a good sense of humour. There was never any formal chat, it was just my dad making crude jokes."

Nevertheless, a twelve-year-old Veronica knew it was private and somewhat shameful ("I was too young to be looking at porn for sure") and with a second-hand phone only for texting, she had to resort to printing out images of Pamela and Leo from the family computer in secret.

I'm not sure of your age, dear reader and what use there is for printing anything now (do the youth still do that? Print stuff?), but the drama of waiting for something to print off that you don't want anyone to see is a very real one. Most people get impatient waiting for their porn to buffer, never mind a slow printer on a dial up internet connection.

Veronica laughs. "I'd be stood there like, 'C'mon, PRINT!'

Then I'd hear my mum coming downstairs and having to pull out the plug and having like a halfway photo." I picture a pair of Pamela's long legs and nothing else. Veronica kept the pictures under her pillow, folded into little squares as if folding them as small as possible would make it more secret. "Mum actually found them. I had a whole bunch of Pamela Anderson photos. But she never talked to me about it. She found them and was like," Veronica pauses, "I can't remember if she was mad or what she said but I think I lost internet privileges. She made it like, a kind of, I think I got punished for it to be honest. Yeah...I think I got punished for it." She giggles, looking off to the side. "And now I like to be punished." I imagine Veronica in the throes of passion: *Take away my internet privileges, yeah, baby!*

The shame didn't seem to scar Veronica. She shrugs. "I had a couple more photos left so I thought to myself, 'I don't care at least I have a couple more to jerk myself to.'"

"Was it the same for Leo?"

"Yeah, but see it wasn't sexual it was romantic with him."

Young Veronica would jerk off to Pamela and imagine her wedding day with Leo.

"Strange, isn't it?" Veronica says. "I still get that way when I'm watching porn now. I don't care too much about the guy and focus on the woman. Even now as an adult when I'm sexual and alone it'll be more female oriented." Before I can chime in, she interrupts herself, stroking her chin and puts on a German accent, imitating Freud, "Zis is very interesting! Zuh self-discovery, Thomasin...I vonder vhat zat's about." Then she ramps up her Valley girl voice to answer her Freud. She whines, "I need both!"

Greedy, as they say.

Veronica started exploring with girls as a teenager, keeping it a deadly secret from anyone else. As gossipy as teenage girls can be, Veronica placed her trust in the right friends, ones with equal amounts to lose if their parents found out, but too bicurious to stop themselves.

"I'd go 'DON'T tell anyone,' and she'd go, 'don't tell ANYONE.' In Canada the grounds of public schools are quite...they can be quite long, we'd have a little forestry bit but during recess we have quite a lot of space to like, go and hide and do stuff and," she says, presenting her hands like a waiter presents a meal to their patrons, "…enjoy! It was between the ages of like, thirteen and fifteen, when you have a little bit more freedom. It happened only with two girls – friends of mine."

They would sneak a cigarette by a stream of water and Veronica would start asking questions.

Have you ever kissed a girl before?

Have you thought about it?

Would you kiss me?

"That sort of rhetoric and 'Oh this is fun.' It was usually quite fun."

I mean, I can understand having a smoke and a cheeky kiss. But full-on heavy petting?

"Yeah like – it all was very gradual. Like first, fingering was around for a couple of years before I went down on someone. Ages fifteen to eighteen I went further. It was quite a study of progression, and then after the age of…I guess Victoria would have been the first time I was fully naked, no adults in the house, I can totally explore, there's no time constraints," she explains, making a flourish with her hands again, "enjoy."

For all the talk of romanticising Leonardo DiCaprio, Victoria was truly Veronica's first love.

"I'd known Victoria since I was a child. I always thought she was so beautiful, and I always wished I'd looked like her.

She was Israeli, she had long blonde hair, tanned skin all year round and had the most beautiful pear-shaped body. Just a really beautiful girl. I love her still." She smiles and says, "I always thought…I couldn't imagine how lucky it would be to be with her. To taste her. When I gained more confidence when I was around seventeen, we were at a party at my house and we just spent the whole night fooling around and like, having sex. It was amazing. And it continued for a little while and then," she stops abruptly, and for a moment I feel like the story will end in heartbreak. She takes a deep breath and continues, "I actually stopped it, 'cos I was like, 'I don't wanna lose you as a friend!' I was too scared 'cos I'd known her for so long, it had been my whole teenage years and I was scared of *actually* losing her if anything went wrong so – and I think she was genuinely just bicurious and just trying things out – so actually she didn't care, she was like, 'Yah, okay fine.' She still laughs about it now! She's almost disappointed, like, 'We could have continued that for a while.'"

It reminds me of Andrew's conundrum, though at least no one was married this time. "It sounds like you were afraid you'd catch feelings."

"Oh yeah. Definitely. I was really worried about it. She's always been my best friend and she still is now. That would have been so distressing if I'd lost that friendship over like, you know, wanting to have sex with her."

I think that's a common worry for boy and girl mates too. I remember as a young teen, my dad told me that he didn't think men and women can truly be friends. I guess he was trying to warn me not to be too friendly back to boys who were friendly with me. "They only want one thing." He didn't explicitly say that, but it was obviously the gist. There would always be some sort of romantic or sexual tension for a man and woman who were emotionally close. It would be inappropriate. I can't actually remember if I refuted it aloud or whether I just thought it in my head, but I do remember the feeling.

So, bisexuals or pansexuals can't be friends with...anyone?

If it had been aloud, I didn't get my answer.

For Veronica, the worry wasn't actually in getting together officially and breaking up like the usual risk that comes with becoming romantic, it was a fear of rejection of her entire sexuality.

"I was more worried that she'd be like, 'I'm not really into girls, I was just sort of trying things out and I don't want to be girlfriends. Like, I'm actually just really straight.'"

"Is she?"

"Well, she's not had any other experiences with women since," Veronica says, and then she bursts out laughing.

Either Veronica is on a Derren Brown level of persuasiveness, dear reader, or Victoria is the most easy-going mate to ever have.

It's funny to me that there's this common idea that bisexual people are 'easy' or oversexed when in this friendship it was Veronica who stopped it for fear of being hurt. Even now, she feels conflicted over what the brief relationship was. "I do wonder if it was performative for her 'cos she was seeing a guy around the time it started and he was really into the fact that she started with girls. So, I always had that in the back of my head that it was performative, and she was relaying stories to him. I'm really glad that now we're closer than ever. We don't see each other much 'cos she's in Canada, but we're really good."

It was thankfully easy to move on; I could paint it as frivolous. Between finishing high school and starting university, Veronica would have formal dates with other girls.

"It would often be with girls who I'd been friends with for a while. We'd be out drinking and I'd be like, 'Oh have you ever considered…?' You know? And they were like, 'Oh, no, but with yooooou? Wink, wink.' On a night out is where the experiences would start and then we'd have a non-platonic relationship for a while until…it was always mutual endings 'cos we were so young. We were like, 'Well that was fun! Let's just continue on.' I didn't come out about it. Like, I wouldn't be telling my nana about it because it was never a big deal to me."

Veronica slept with her first boy at eighteen. Was this the beginning of her romantic life? A whole new, deeper experience after the frivolity of heavy petting her school friends? Well, not quite. Veronica was not impressed, and for a few years wondered whether she was gay. She loved men romantically and had crushes, but struggled to have the same sexual intensity as she'd had with women.

"I always thought men were such *bad kissers*. Foreplay was always like EWWWWWWW. This is so NOT NICE. And I realised that women are quite wet and soft and men can be kinda like," she splutters, trying to find the right word, "dry?! And stiff. Weirdly *stiff*. But generally, I've had deeper expectations and romantic feelings in men, and I think that often does translate to a more intense experience."

So that's Veronica, at least up until she walks into Dante's *Inferno*.

F
  L
   A
    S
     H
      B
       A
        C
        K

And now she's being invited to a threesome with a relationship therapist and a ballerina. Over text. "I really quickly chickened out. I was like, "'AHUHIDUNNO I really can't.' And I explained that while I had experience with women, I'd never had *that* sort of experience and it's, it's a lot. I really expressed my anxieties over it to them and they were so kind that I remember having second thoughts, 'Wow, is it wrong of me to not give these two kind, sweet people a chance? They've not really shown me anything bad. The only thing wrong is they've not really given up.'"

As British as it sounds, Veronica kept messaging them out of sheer politeness.

"They kept asking if I'd given their threesome idea any more thought. It would happen a lot. Eventually I was like fuck it 'cos he said – no she said – or he said," she flaps her hands, waving away the cloud of confusion, "I mean either one of them 'cos it's kind of like, like they're a unit at this point to me, 'let's go to your favourite restaurant.'" Veronica chose an Italian restaurant tucked away on Marylebone Lane. "It's a little bit overpriced but it's really cute."

Forget politeness, now Veronica is being convinced into a date because it means a free dinner at Caldezzi's; what an endorsement.

Caldezzi's!

So good you'll contemplate a threesome.

Veronica, Relationship Therapist and Ballerina meet there, eat two courses, and drink a lot of wine. The talk is civil. It's only around 10 pm when the first bottle of wine is finished that the mood shifts. "Suddenly there was no one in the restaurant, and it was just our group of three in the top level and just waiters every now and again. And then I remember he goes, 'Why don't you kiss her?' And so, I kissed her in the restaurant, in front of him. And then maybe I kissed him. But I don't remember anything with him, I remember with her. And one thing led to another and suddenly I was in the backseat and we're driving home."

Veronica and Ballerina are in the backseat with Relationship Therapist, at the wheel, giving prompts. "It was strange, I did feel like we were sort of just following what he was asking but I was really keen anyway. But the dynamic was strange. He was saying, 'Why don't you lick it?' I was like, 'Tee hee okay bleublueuelbleu.' Oh fuck, I wish I could remember their names. I'm terrible."

Despite her attraction to Ballerina, Veronica begins to feel uneasy, the red wine stirring in her stomach as the car speeds across London.

"I'd only had experiences with single women and single men and even that was quite juvenile 'cos I was still pretty young at the time. It was more like discovering and exploring the body rather than having really explorative sex with women, you know? I remember feeling uncomfortable 'cos he was drinking, and we were on the motorway going back to Wimbledon and we weren't wearing seatbelts."

"*Veronica!*" I tut, the most appalled I've been in any interview yet.

"Well, we were eating each other out in the backseat like totally full on. And fingering!" Veronica is trying to explain

215

the situation physically on the coffee shop sofa. The staff look over just as she's miming the fingering, and for a moment, I think we're about to be told to fuck off out of Fuckoffee. But they're unbothered and turn away as Veronica finishes her demonstration.

"Well, you can't wear seatbelts for that," I conclude.

Veronica brought them back to her student house ("I felt safer. There's no way I'm gonna go to theirs"). It was a strange clashing of worlds as mature Relationship Therapist and elegant Ballerina floated through a house full of unopened post addressed to previous students, second-hand Ikea furniture and a fridge full of three separate cartons of milk (one with sharpie lines all the way up it to measure that no one was stealing from it). And into the bedroom.

"I put them in the room, and I went to the bathroom to put some cold water on my face and gave myself a pep talk. 'This is happening, you've brought them here now.'"

So, it's happening. She's committed. The wine is really starting to give her belly ache now and she could sort of go to sleep, but Veronica is about to have a threesome. She makes a game plan about how to initiate it. Perhaps setting the right lighting? Perhaps changing into some sexy lingerie? Not that she has any of that. But she has a sexy nurse Halloween costume from fresher's week stuffed in the back of her wardrobe, maybe that would work?! Or maybe just taking things slow and natural.

"I was in there freshening up for only two minutes and I came back and Thomasin – they're BOTH naked and already started. I think he was licking her and sucking her boobs or something. They were full on in the midst of foreplay and I'm there fully dressed like, 'Okay. This is horrible.' I mean they *started without me!*"

I didn't know that could happen in threesomes. Very rude guests! Of course, I'm not one to understand threesome etiquette, dear reader, but I'm pretty sure all three have to be there at the start line. What did she do? Is she thinking, 'I better get naked and tag in?'

"Pretty much. I went up to the bed a bit like, 'Yoo hoo, remember me?' And they hesitated and then kissed me, there was like, a brief moment where they allowed me to take my clothes off."

"I really felt like I was intruding at that point and that's where it was surprising 'cos I hadn't felt that way up until that point at all. I'd been courted and seduced. Now I was being ignored."

What about the sex itself?

"I focused on her. 'Cos I realised I really wasn't attracted to him physically and I don't think there was much of him and me going on at all. I'm pretty sure I ignored him. It was strange, both of us focusing on her. And she was asking me to do things very rough." Veronica launches into a posh, clipped accent and adds, "She was like, 'Slap me! On my BUM! Slap me on my bum. Okay harder.' 'Uhalright.' Then she's like correcting me like, 'No, no put TWO fingers in.' I'm just giving awkward replies like, 'Okey dokey, no problemo!' I was just trying to appease and maybe placate at this stage, I don't think I was enjoying much of the situation. It wasn't a sexy experience. It wasn't very passionate, and I didn't like that. And then of course they fell asleep. And I," she stops again, putting her head in her hands, "I didn't expect them to *sleep over*. 'Cos I've got housemates and stuff! It was around midnight. I did feel like they could have maybe…I guess they thought, 'Nah Wimbledon's too far out, we better sleep over.' And then I woke up to them having sex next to me. AGAIN!"

We both have our head in our hands now, side by side in Fuckoffee. "Oh Veronica…"

"Again in the morning! Not just without me but next to my sleeping body. And I CAN HEAR MY HOUSEMATES DOWNSTAIRS THIS WHOLE TIME. Hearing ALL of it. And I just thought, 'This is NOT hot.' It ALMOST was, it really was QUITE sexy and then it wasn't. I mean, the build-up was really quite intriguing. The sex was the least exciting part. But the worst part really was after."

Compelled once again by politeness, Veronica sent them a text full of pleasant lies. "'Thank you so much for that experience, I hope you guys are good, maybe we'll see each other again.' Even though I didn't really want to, I just thought that whatever happened at least it's a good story. I got a message from the guy immediately." She goes back into her Vin Diesel voice, "'Guuuuh so amazing, you're beautiful! Hope you're feeling good.' It was actually a really nice, empowering message from him. And I got *nothing* from her. A couple of days later I got a private message from her saying that she had a really bad time."

Oh shit.

But it's not what you think. "She thought I was more experienced than I came off and that I hadn't pleased her. She made me feel really clumsy. It was so strange. In retrospect I think it was probably the first time they did it and they pretended it wasn't themselves. So, they were hoping for an experienced third party."

"Wow. I can't believe she gave you feedback," I say. Though I can believe it; that's such a dancer's attitude. She

219

gave performance notes. "You were behind the beat on this section, so maybe go away and practice before the next run?"

Veronica shrugs. "I don't think it was notes, I think it was a review. She made it clear there wouldn't be a next time. I think it was along the lines of, 'that's why I won't be seeing you again.' I never saw her again, but it wasn't the last time I heard from the guy. I think I even asked him about it and he was like, 'Naaaaaaah don't worry about it.' He brushed it off. 'It's fine.' He was great in that way. I ignored him during all of it so if anything I expected *him* to be annoyed."

I raise my eyebrows. To be honest, I think he was probably thinking he'd pushed his luck far enough and was just happy to be there. But I don't say that.

"And he was a relationship therapist?" I ask. "Are you *sure?*"

Veronica grimaces. "Well, that's what he said."

I try to find him, to try and make sense of this man. I feel like any relationship therapist would advise against dating a teenager for a start. It's very difficult without a name though. I'm telling you, dear reader, I look everywhere and nothing comes up! And by 'everywhere' I mean the first page of Google. But 'Greek relationship therapist in London published book circus analogies' doesn't get you much besides a change to your ad algorithm. I get a lot of therapy stuff now. Searching for stuff on the internet is nerve-racking. Big Brother is truly with us, and I don't like my searches to be recorded because I know I search for random shit. I was once doing a standup joke about people being too obsessed with their horoscope but through the lens of Putin. So, I found myself googling 'What star sign is Putin?' And because I didn't then want my computer to think I was pro-Putin, I immediately started to Google a bunch of other random things like 'Would Jesus have been good at playing the piano?' And 'Why are Parrots such cunts?'

Now older, Veronica feels the creep factor of the encounter a lot more. "I'm like, 'Oof, that was some weird vibes.'" But she was of course not much older than a teenager herself, and with a large age gap with her own parents it was difficult to grasp the real power dynamic between the couple. "I even felt a responsibility 'cos Ballerina was that little bit younger than me and at that age it can feel like a lot, like, 'I've been through my first year at uni, I know what that feels like and you're just starting. You've got a lot to learn you young one.'"

"Do you think maybe if you just met her at a bar and she'd shown interest, do you think it would have gotten that far?"

Veronica looks at the loud art on the walls of Fuckoffee, searching for an answer. "I mean, if it had stopped after we met the first time in Quebec then I'd say yes. But after how it concluded I'd say probably not. I would say that she was the conduit for his intention, you know? Oh, that sounds horrible. Maybe not. Maybe I'm remembering it wrong.

'Cos I don't remember her as well as I remember him now. I was hurt, so I think I blocked out what she was like."

So that's her one story. Veronica has since had more experiences with women, a lot more easy, a lot more straightforward, but not very exciting sexually. As she's grown up, the tables have turned. "I've had much more sexually exciting experiences with men since, which is probably why I've ended up dating more men as I get older. I'd be with – I hate this word – I'd be with *straight passing* women who'd maybe not had experiences themselves with women, so they're asking, 'Can I touch this? Can I kiss you like this?' Like a lot of asking for permission, which is great etiquette, but there wouldn't be much of that unspoken dialogue. It's less thrilling, less satisfying for me."

Veronica is now married, she met her husband on a cruise ship and they spent a few years on the job together, but before then she was exclusively dating men for a few years. "I was gonna meet up with a couple of promising women but then I chickened out 'cos of that Ballerina experience. I felt too vulnerable and sensitive to give that a proper go again. I mean I did a little, I've enjoyed some things and even helping other women realise that part of themselves. But I've not properly dated any women. I did consider it, but then I only set my dating app for men. I also didn't feel like having anything too complicated, like it would open a can of worms emotionally to date women again. I thought, 'I'm just going to go back to good old faithful dick.'"

It is a theme I've seen come up for people who define themselves as bisexual but choose long-term relationships with the opposite gender. It *is* less complicated. Is that chickening out? Are you still allowed to comment on queer culture as if you're part of it? Or are you going to be like the annoying straight hen party causing chaos in the gay club? Hell, what gives me the audacity to even write a book on it? And in all honesty, it's not biphobic to say it's easier as a woman to be with a guy because it just is. You're fed the narrative from a young age. As Ros said, it's in the coding, in the body language all around you. You kind of know what to do, or at least what it's expected to look like. Taylor Swift tells you all about it. Life imitates art. And if you do like men, why go against the grain? Just stick to good old faithful dick. But stay there. Stay there and don't talk about your other feelings, don't bring up anything that diverges and *certainly* don't write a book about it as a way to indirectly come out to your nan.

Things also changed as Veronica got older; suddenly she had to consider settling down with a partner. "I'd never thought about it properly, but I knew I'd never want a future with a woman, like a wife and living in a house with a woman and no children. I mean, having a biological child would be really difficult at least. So, I ruled it out. I want a husband and *lots* of babies. So suddenly any connection to a woman was just fooling around. And then if that wasn't satisfying me sexually, there wasn't much point. Maybe if I was ever single again, I'd revisit that side of myself, now that I'm older and wiser. Who knows?"

I have a theory for Veronica. I wonder if being able to sleep with more mature and experienced men as she's gotten older has also changed things. "Do you feel now that it's better sex with guys, the less need you feel to experience women? Were you just after good sex all along?"

Veronica folds her arms thoughtfully. "Hmm. Maybe I was just after good, passionate sex. Always after a good connection. Maybe in that sense, gender doesn't really matter too much." Pamela or Leo, a wank's a wank.

"I mean I really do wonder sometimes if I should revisit it somehow but I haven't felt much attraction to women I've met in the past few years compared to in my teens or early twenties. I always said I'm bisexual just because of how many women I dated in my teens and like exclusively I really, really enjoyed going out and messing around with boys or girls equally. It was *extremely* equal up until the age of about twenty-three. But now? You could say I never was, you could call it bicuriousity, because I think bisexuality is something that is with you forever. I don't know, I haven't really given it much thought lately. Like I wonder how I would label myself, if I had to. I hate using the word 'phase' 'cos I don't want it to affect those that it's not a phase for, is there a better word? I feel bad. But I shouldn't, right?"

I wonder if Veronica will tell her children. "I think if they ask, I'd tell them. But I can't imagine them asking – do you ask your parents about what they were up to when they were younger? I'm pretty sure everything my parents told me they did as teenagers was against my will. 'I used to listen to this band' or 'I remember life before the internet.' So, I'm not too worried as I don't really see that happening. Maybe when they're grown-ups, or if they have their own stuff they want to talk through, and it helps."

Whatever the future holds, Veronica's chapter with women is finished. "I don't see myself with another partner so that won't be an issue. If, say, touch wood," we tap on the table simultaneously, "something happened to my husband, and I was widowed, I would want another partner. He'd want that for me too. And I think for the sake of the kids I would be looking for a long-term male partner. I just think that would be easier on everyone. Including me! Like, it's what I'd want, I think. It's what I've wanted for a long time now."

It's interesting to see her preferences change over time. I think this is why so many people see bisexuality as a phase; it's because for so many people it legitimately is. Or maybe it's not, maybe you're always bisexual but your sexual preferences evolve over time anyway. I mean, that's the same thing for straight women, isn't it? You don't always fancy the same sort of people at thirteen as you do at fifty. Bald men with beards were kind of gross to me when I was fifteen but now it's very alluring. I'm still straight but I'd rather bonk Gimli than Legolas (I think it's the Scottish accent that's doing it for me).

We conclude the conversation with a mutual shrug. *We don't have the answers, only our experiences.*

Veronica met me today, putting her trust in an internet stranger and poured her heart out about many things, including a story where her trust in strangers led her down a very weird path indeed. But she's alright – great in fact. And I realise that above all she has trust in herself. She shakes her head when I describe all my feelings of being 'weird' growing up.

"It's not weird though. I think it's quite normal to experiment with your own gender." She smiles and concludes, "Many people will visit Maple Wine Cellar, but they don't have to go all the way to the basement floor like I did. They still go in…Yes, I think it's very, very normal."

CHAPTER 11:
TWO BROTHERS

In many ways, Carl is a man of contradictions (and complaints).

Carl trained in IT but works with his hands. ("It just didn't pan out.")

Carl *loves* film but avoids the cinema. ("It's a weird atmosphere since the pandemic – too many people with their shoes off.")

Carl is an introvert, but his first kiss with a boy was on a stranger's bed in front of a cheering crowd.

Out of all the interviewees so far, Carl is someone that I know the least, and we've only ever seen each other via Zoom. I couldn't even tell you how tall he is. He appears on camera with a sensible haircut, glasses and a round face. He is a childhood friend of an old work colleague of mine called Freddie, a singer who likes to introduce himself as, "'Freddie the singer' – not the one you deserve but maybe the one you need." I guess that's a reference to the late Freddie Mercury (and maybe also Batman?) and at the mention of Freddie Mercury, we bring up the film *Bohemian Rhapsody*.

Carl is very reserved, but there's a fire underneath and it comes to life as we discuss the film.

"It is the most insulting recent mainstream depiction of bisexuality I've seen yet," he practically spits out. "It totally dismissed Freddie Mercury's bisexuality until it could be lumped into his drug-fuelled downfall as though it was something audiences should feel ashamed about. Seriously, fuck that poorly edited bullshit film."

I suck my teeth loudly to fill the awkward silence that follows. "Yeah, but did you like it?"

So, I am a huge Queen fan, like, *huge*. Like go-to-Montreaux-specifically-to-see-the-Freddie-Mercury-statue-huge. The unpopular school nerd that still lurks in me finds a strange solidarity in that band – I think that's its appeal really. Somewhere in that huge rock 'n' roll mythos of John Deacon, Roger Taylor, Brian May and the late Freddie Mercury were just three science geeks and their weird art goth friend. They drove fast cars, did drugs, fucked around A LOT and performed to thousands, but you felt that somehow you could relate to them. They've always been popular, but they've always been a little uncool. They were misfits playing for other misfits. The only reason I haven't seen the film is I've read too many biographies and have probably ruined the experience for myself. The talented cast could be rocking out to *Fat Bottomed Girls*, and I'd be sat there quietly saying, "but this scene is set in 1974 and that song wasn't released until 1979." I actually worked with Brian May (very briefly) on a theatre gig a few years ago, but I was too shy to barely look his way, let alone have a chat or get a photo. Letting him get away without making a bashful idiot of myself is my biggest lifelong regret alongside that time in 2014 when I got a fringe. I'm serious, dear reader, I fucking love Queen. John Deacon could punch me in the face, and I would thank him for his time.

Anyway, despite this, I don't say anything to add to Carl's ruthless review. Frankly I'm just happy to see some life in him. These exciting outbursts happen rarely in the interview, but when they do I see a passionate man. Carl will talk slowly, a little vaguely, and then suddenly he'll spring to life. Mostly though, he seems anxious to be interviewed, which is understandable; he's protective of the humble life he's built in the small town of Stalham. He's especially protective when we bring up his girlfriend, Grace.

"I told Grace a few years back that I was bisexual, and she didn't know how to react. But she is…Um." He stops, unsure of how much to divulge. "She is…we have had an open conversation and she is more, erm, accepting. And understanding. And that feels good. And I did tell an odd couple of old friends too while I was drunk, including Freddie." He raises his eyebrows, almost surprised at himself as he looks back. "I don't know why, probably because one of the guys was bi, so I felt like I could confide in him and just be open about it. And my friends have been so welcoming about it. But before then I was talking with another friend who I found out was also bisexual, and he said to me, 'If you're worried about telling someone, then maybe it's for a good reason, so it's probably better you don't tell them.' Something like that. And I just really, I took that in. I took those words to heart for a while. But thankfully my friends have all reacted well so far, and it's just been really heartwarming."

Carl's parents are Portuguese and moved to the UK just before he was born. "My parents never bothered to teach me the language; I guess they wanted me to fit in." Carl was raised in Folkestone in a working-class household, but at aged ten the family relocated to Norfolk for more job opportunities and it's where he's lived ever since. Now aged twenty-three, Carl works in a warehouse that builds equipment for hospitals. It pays the bills. His real passion is in film critique, and he has his own podcast and YouTube channel with a small but consistent audience of listeners.

Carl quietly slipped into the crowd at school. Not a standout, but not a loser. He reflects on the way he looks. "My skin is a bit darker than the majority of the pale white kids I grew up with. I think people knew I was different. But when you're a kid Pokémon is more interesting than where this person is from. It wasn't until secondary school where people made more jokes about me being Portuguese – at my expense."

Carl's not sure at what age he started noticing girls, but he remembers early on that there was the expectation that he should. "I think heterosexuality is one of those things that parents kind of, whether intentionally or not, instil in you when you're younger, so it's an..."—his voice goes high pitched, impersonating his mum—"'Ohhh is she your girl-friend? Ohh he's shy.' It's those little things that make you think, 'Everyone's saying it, I suppose I need to get on with it. Quick! Show some interest in a girl or something!'"

I feel for Carl; I definitely felt that pressure growing up, I think it all went downhill for me when my mum got Sky installed and we had access to all these channels like Nickel-odeon and the Disney Channel just as I hit those formative tween years. All that American media depicting the rich girls in California, talking on flip cell phones and going to the mall with their gal pals. I felt like such a failure with my fat Nokia brick phone and not being allowed to even walk down to the local shop by myself because I was, as my mum put it, 'away with the Fairies.' (Stupid. She meant stupid.) And all they talked about on those shows were the boys. How are we gonna impress the boys? Where are the boys? Will there be booooys at the party? Which boy do you LIKE like? I used to think, 'I don't know what kind of boys you run into Mary-Kate and Ashley, but the boys at my school are fucking bellends. Even the cute ones.' And I don't mean that in a horrible way, they were twelve-year-old kids. At that age, dear reader, are we not all bellends, in our own individual ways?

Back to Carl, growing up he understood the concept of "boys liking boys, girls like girls" – but by his notion, he'd never expected it was something that could happen to him.

"I didn't really actually think about liking a boy until I was about fourteen. There was this guy in my class called Milo who was so confident – everybody liked him. He was always cracking jokes and was so unapologetic about it. Not in the way of 'dickhead who says racist things.' I mean in like, a self-confident way. It just made me go." He pauses, pretending to look someone up and down and says quietly. "Hello."

Carl had intense feelings about Milo, but they were never acted upon. "And then I just brushed it off because well, I'm still finding myself and that was still something which made me think, 'No, no, no, they say go for girls so go for girls.'"

It sounds to me like Carl realised he had an authentic attraction for boys before any real feelings for girls developed.

Carl thinks. "I mean, I did fall for girls. I did. I had an attraction for maybe two or one in early secondary school. Or late primary school."

"Did you have a girlfriend?" I ask.

"I was awkward," Carl replies.

I didn't know that was an option when answering that question.

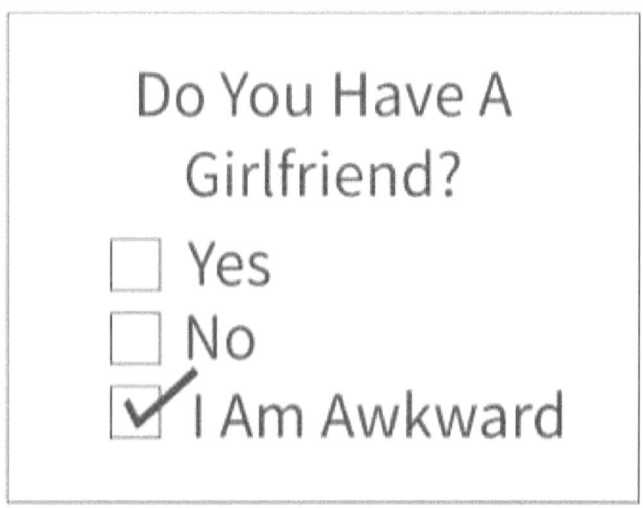

Do You Have A
Girlfriend?
☐ Yes
☐ No
☑ I Am Awkward

Carl actually did have a girlfriend in primary school, around the age of ten. Holding hands and a few pecks in the playground, the usual stuff. Carl could be an angry child, so after getting irritated one too many times and then taking it out on her, she wanted nothing to do with him. "I don't blame her. I was a fucking shit as a kid. If something didn't go my way, I'd make a pouty face, fold my arms and be a bit like, 'No, I don't LIKE you anymore.' I wasn't one of those kids who chucked things or had a tantrum and broke things…I just wasn't as clean cut as I'd like to have been."

"That's just kids though, isn't it?" I say. I'm trying to make him feel better, but I can tell by his reaction that he thinks I'm downplaying his feelings.

"Hmmmmyeah," he mumbles, looking off into the distance, which clearly translates as a mature adult version of, 'No, you're wrong. I don't LIKE you anymore.'

After a while, Carl's feelings for Milo evolved into a friendship. "I was happy just being his friend. I never tried anything. I did have feelings about other boys, but it was nothing. I had a laugh with them in the way you do when your class is together, and there's no teacher, and you're just having fun. I made a point not to hang out with them after school."

Carl is a late bloomer. He got his first and so far, only girlfriend at nineteen, Grace. They've been together for nearly five years. I congratulate him on the longevity; many couples grow apart rather than grow together at his age.

"Thank you," he says. "People like to think of relationships as sweeping romances."

I think he's going to go on to say more but he doesn't. We look at each other expectantly.

"Anyhoo," I say.

Carl met Grace at the party of a mutual friend. "We both got drunk and started making out."

"Tale as old as time," I say wistfully.

"Mmhmm."

Carl went to work the early shift the next day at Sainsburys, hung over. It wasn't pleasant, but he found himself light on his feet, unable to keep Grace out of his mind. The aisles of Sainsburys suddenly became the most beautiful place on earth.

Carl and Grace lived within walking distance of each other, and they became inseparable. Now they've been living together for three years. Unlike Zain, Carl has remained faithful to Grace, and his bisexuality has gone unexplored. And unlike Ros, ethical non-monogamy is not for them. So, his many explorations happened at sixth form. And there they'll stay.

"I was about seventeen. And there was a house party with some people I went to college with – just standard 'get pissed and debauchery' kind of thing."

A house party. A mixture of girls, boys. Alcohol. No parents – though the host's sensible older brother is there keeping watch. The host's name is Cameron, a smiley daredevil with dyed punk red hair, loose vest tops to show off his toned arms and the kind of guy that gets along with everyone, despite the extreme look.

"Cameron and I were in classes together in college. So, I knew him. He was another of those, like, cracking jokes, self-confident, kind of guys." He then says abruptly, as if realising it for the first time, "Jesus Christ, I have a type!"

The party isn't just his sixth form pals, but former secondary school students who Carl hasn't seen for a few

235

months, the ones that used to make him the butt of the jokes. "I was a bit, well, a lot more introverted than I am now. So, it was a case of, 'Yeah, I'm gonna do this. I'm gonna have a fun time.' Step out of my zone a bit. A lot of it was just sitting around chatting and listening to the music, having some beers – and I don't like beer, so you can tell I was trying to fit in."

Determined to have fun and assert himself in front of his ex-bullies, Carl impresses Cameron. They get drunk together, they joke together. They talk and talk. Way more than they've ever done at school.

"Do you remember what you talked about?" I ask.

Carl shakes his head; it was irrelevant. "It was just drunken talk; that talk where it's essentially about nothing but you're trying to make it out as though it is something. A lot of it I don't remember. But we were hanging out together. And I do remember there was a load of, erm, raucous people upstairs. There was a few of us and just like, chatting shit, having fun. The music was really loud, lots of crappy rap, pop songs like Black Eyed Peas which are popular at the time, but ten years later, you're like, 'Jesus Christ, people like that?'"

I also like Black Eyed Peas (or maybe I'm just crushing hard on Fergie) but I realise now is not the time to make a case for them.

Carl and Cameron head upstairs. People are randomly hanging out in Cameron's parents' bedroom, standing around the empty double bed and shiny cheap throw pillows. "And then at some point, Cameron and I were like, 'let's kiss, let's go for it!' And it's not like a quick peck. It's a full-on snog."

Surrounded by a crowd of cheering and laughing teenagers and the surreal but distinct sound of *The Fresh Prince of Bel Air* coming on the shuffle, Carl lays down on the bed and has his first romantic kiss with a boy.

It's pretty wild for an introverted, sometimes bullied teenage boy. Carl shrugs. "We were both drunk. We just laughed and moved on. But I think that was definitely me taking a step. And for me, just kind of – even if I didn't admit it to myself out loud – it was me confirming inside, 'Yeah. This is how I feel. This is real.'"

Despite the buzz it created with their friends, Carl wasn't worried. Not in the habit of sharing much with his parents, he had no worries of his family finding out. And Cameron never brought it up again, but it was a feeling that lingered on in Carl for years after.

I wonder what happened between Carl and Cameron after that?

"Not much. He dropped out of sixth form and got his new girlfriend pregnant."

I gasp, "Oh no, Cameron!"

"We lost touch. There was a bit of a sour instance, which, which essentially just made, I don't want to go into it," he says sharply, angrily even. It alarms me. "But essentially it just made me think I don't want him in my life, and I just want to move on. I blocked him everywhere online."

It's clear that there's a lot being left unsaid, and although I try to gently prod some more, Carl's not giving it up. Not every story gets to be told. Carl, however, brings up a story that, I suspect, might have something to do with their falling out.

"Later on, at that same party, I got chatting with Cameron's older brother, Danny, you know, the older, sensible brother watching over the party? Danny's a gay man, and we got chatting."

"I think the thing was that his brother was a bit more," he looks up, searching for the word, "I don't want to say straightlaced. Because he wasn't. But he was definitely no-where near as wild or…"

Yes? I think. Wild or…?

Handsome?

Sexy?

Irresponsible?

"Yeah," he affirms, and for a moment I panic that Zoom is transmitting my thoughts across to him out loud. (God, how bad would that be if that was a hidden feature of Zoom that everyone's unaware of, like the vanity filter?)

"He was open about who he was," Carl continues, "so I think it was probably that which may have gotten my inter-est."

Danny dressed more modestly than Cameron, sporting a buzzcut, notably thinner. "But there was a resemblance in the face," Carl says.

"Is there a part of you that went for Danny because he looked like Cameron? Because they sound like polar oppo-sites in personality."

Carl's frowns. He's not sure. "It wasn't a conscious deci-sion," he concludes.

Danny befriended Carl, and they talked over the course of nearly all of Carl's school year, flirting on social media. They also met up at a couple more house parties, even kiss-ing at some – and in private, this time. The performative, jokey atmosphere that Carl could fall back on to kiss Cam-eron was gone. Suddenly it was too real.

"I broke it off because I was probably feeling shame or something. But it was just, I remember, there was a lot of build-up, and we were like, friendly. And there was a bit of tension between us. But when we had a kiss at this party in the darkened room away from other people, I just knew."

Sensing that Danny wanted to go further than kissing, Carl pushed him away. At seventeen, Carl was still a virgin and had little experience in anything further. Feeling that he was at a crossroads, Carl made a choice.

"I said no, no, no, I don't want to follow through with this. And I think that was just me being scared about the fact that if I follow through, if this guy is my first then I, I just don't want that. There's no coming back from it. And I think it was more, like as much as I knew inside that I was bi, I was desperate not to confirm it and to just move on."

Was Danny just a placeholder for Cameron, the person he really wanted but couldn't have? Or was he a gay man that Carl had the opportunity to explore more of his sexuality with? Or was it deeper, did he actually have feelings for him?

Carl's sure of this answer, and full of regret: "I did have feelings for him. Yeah." And he sounds full of regret for ever letting himself get there.

Thankfully, Danny didn't push the vulnerable Carl to go further, but the messages stopped not long after. Feeling used and embarrassed, Carl eventually blocked him.

And that's where Carl's story ends – for now. He is young, and still has a journey ahead of him, but his commitment to Grace means that any further consummation of his bisexuality is off the cards. I think it's important to include stories like his in my book, dear reader. Coming to terms with his sexual identity and understanding of who he is has been fundamental to his growth and kept his relationship strong. I don't think any lack of experience should take that away. A bisexual man who stays with one woman is still a bisexual. You don't tell a single man he's asexual just because he's not currently with a woman, do you? So, it's the same here. Perhaps you're thinking, 'What does it bloody matter then, if they're in a long term heterosexual relationship? Why feel the need to be so open about being bisexual? Why did you pick this story?' After so many wild stories of threesomes and cheating, I wanted to include something more 'mundane' because sometimes that's also what bisexuality is. And the more open we all are about this, the easier it will be for future seventeen-year-old lads wanting to act on those impulses to feel that they can. Even if they end up with a girl who makes their heart skip a beat as they walk down the aisle of Sainsburys, why should the path up to that be filled with shame? Carl is in a good place now, but that shame he felt over Cameron and Danny lingered to the point that he waited years to admit it to the woman he loved that he'd been hiding a part of himself.

I wave goodbye to Carl, and he exits the Zoom chat. I stare at my face in the Zoom webcam, trying to process his story, trying to find an angle. God, I hope he and Grace are happy, but in all honesty I don't know. Weirdly, I find myself thinking of Freddie Mercury again. I haven't seen the film *Bohemian Rhapsody*, so it's hard to comment on Carl's critique. As an avid Queen fan, however, it does strike me that Freddie was a contradiction, much like Carl. One minute in interviews saying, "I'll fuck anyone" or describing himself as being as gay "as a daffodil," to avoiding the press like the plague and any discussion of the kind. He was famous for his lack of interviews and protection over his private life. I guess information didn't get around as easily as it does now with new media, because although the press often described him as bisexual, many Queen fans assumed he was straight. His bandmates outright lied on his behalf to journalists who asked if their lead singer was gay, "Not to my knowledge" or "let's change the subject." I wonder whether Freddie said such bombastic things in interviews as part of the act. Perhaps it seemed more acceptable for him to have slept with men (as long as he also said he slept with women) if it was all part of this rock'n'roll partying persona. I don't know if he'd have been so wild if he had become a simple graphic designer and married a girl. Freddie did love women, including Barbara Valentin, with her giant personality and giant tits. But like for Andrew or Steve, I guess it was easier to get access to a bunch of horny men. And maybe more fun. Some claim he's gay icon, some claim he's a bi icon (a bicon, if you will). And then I find myself thinking, does it matter either way? If he's an icon to you then let him be, by all means. But if Freddie Mercury didn't want to define his sexuality to the public, what place have we got trying to 'figure it out' over here? And I think there's a lesson in that. Some people are loud and proud about their sexuality and swing naked from chandeliers, some people just want to fuck around in private and then chill out with their cats. And sometimes they feel like doing one or the other.

Maybe that's a contradiction, but in some ways, us bisexuals are a bit of a contradiction in how different the people we have the capacity to be attracted to are. It's hard to see the rules and boundaries – no wonder historically we've been accused of being perverts. But that's just being human, isn't it, dear reader? Straight, gay, bi or something else, humans have always been a messy, ever-changing combination of opposing ideas. It's not bad, it's not good, it just is. Freddie Mercury can be a gay icon, a bicon or anything you want him to be to you. I really don't think he'd mind. So go easy on me. Go easy on Carl. And go easy on 2018 Musical Drama film *Bohemian Rhapsody*.

CHAPTER 12:
UNITED STATES OF
BISEXUALS

Sammie James swoops into the Zoom chat under the name 'The Demon Lady Lord of the Damned.'

"I was a demon for an online Halloween-themed standup show," she explains with a cheeky, crooked smile. There's nearly always a corner of a smile forming on Sammie's mouth whenever she speaks, like she's on the verge of laughing at whatever she says. It gives even our serious topics of conversation a sitcom sort of sheen. She has large, brown eyes made even larger behind her glasses that make her incredibly expressive. With skin as white as snow and hair as dark as ebony, the tall and willowy Sammie could almost be the androgynous, high-fashion older sibling of Snow White. Their voice is bright and projecting out from my laptop. Despite the blotchy Zoom Wi-Fi that cuts in and out over our chat, Sammie's infectiously positive energy is undeniable.

A fellow standup comedian, Sammie is from New Jersey in the USA. During the winter lockdown of 2020 I decided to join an online US comedy sketch course. Usually, the end of course showcase would be in some Off-Off-Broadway Theatre but seeing as it was now online, I was able to join in and create my own sketch all the way from my bedroom in the UK. We had to write an original sketch and bring it to our online Zoom classes for critique. Later on, we'd film the sketch in bits and pieces and then edit it together for us and an audience to watch on this online showcase. My sketch was about someone doing an online dance workout as a fun and easy way to get fit but the peppy dance instructor on YouTube goes from encouraging to sadistic. The dance instructor would shock the person in the video by randomly going into splits or bringing out their tap shoes while the poor person tried to follow along. It kept getting more and more ridiculous with the dance instructor suddenly appearing with a male partner to do tricks or outfit changes that the person finds impossible to replicate. It ends with a human sacrifice.

I initially envisioned myself as the person trying to follow along with the instructor but as soon as Sammie read the part with her large expressive eyes staring in incredulity at the dance instructor, I knew the role was hers. We shot the sketch and added each other on socials, but that was the last time we spoke. It's now the post-Halloween of the year I'm writing this when I summon The Demon Lady Lord of the

Damned. We're literally worlds apart with a giant ocean between us, but I feel so much more relaxed talking to them over Zoom than to poor Carl recently. But saying that, my confidence is knocked. Carl was pleasant enough, but stand-offish and even defensive when I'd try to get deeper on certain topics. I don't want to end another interview talking about a rock star we all know, I want to talk about Sammie. So, I try to ease in. I ask how the show went.

She answers brightly, "It was good!" Then nothing.

"Nice, nice. MmmMMmm."

Before the awkward silence I anticipate is coming, I try telling a funny anecdote about my own Halloween experience this year. I LOVE Halloween and told my boyfriend Harry that I wanted to go clubbing. Harry is not a dancer, but we were keen to spend the night together. "There will be dancing!" I declared. "Do not come if you're not going to dance. You better be dancing!"

"Alright, but don't make a big deal of it," he mumbled. True to his word, he did commit to some decent swaying on the dance floor. But for the majority of the time his version of dancing was to move his arms like pulling levers on a tractor for about five seconds and then coming close to make out. Admittedly that was still very fun but for an avid *Strictly* watcher like me, dancing is a profession, not foreplay. I dance like a lunatic. I like *space*. I'm ~~like~~ a drunk aunt who wants to try moshing for the first time. Unless there's space for me to *consider* a cartwheel (without actually ever having the intention of doing one), I'm not interested.

So, I'm dressed as a witch for the party, wearing a black steampunk dress, dark purple wig and matching lipstick and with a witch's hat placed delicately on top to complete the picture. Harry comes in a suit straight from work and with a *No Costume No Entry* policy, I hastily placed my witch's hat on his head to gain entry. Without my witchy hat, I spend most of the night looking like I'm appropriating a goth girl.

As I'm queueing at the bar, a guy dressed as a giant foot gestures to my outfit and asks, "What are you?"

"Sexy, duh," I say, putting my hand on my hip and doing a sassy pose. Giant Foot Man looks at me like I'm a Giant Idiot. Oh well, not as bad as a few years ago when I tried to go as a giant spider. I stuck all these plastic black legs to the same black dress but the legs came out looking a bit short and stocky, so I just looked like Queen of the Dildos™.

"…So yeah, all that was a bit of a fail!" I finish the ~~rambling~~ story to Sammie. I can't tell if it's the bad Wi-Fi connection that prevented the story from making much sense. (I just picture me starting by talking about enjoying Halloween, followed by the Zoom freezing for thirty seconds and it coming back just as I'm declaring "Queen of the Dildos!") Either way, Sammie doesn't really react.

"So yeaaaaah," I say in a singsong voice. "Halloween was goooood."

Sammie talks about The Demon Lady Lord of the Damned, "I'm mostly a standup and storyteller but I've been getting into character in the last few years."

"I want to see what your Demon sounds like!" I say.

Sammie smiles through the Zoom camera. Nothing.

Wow, this is going so well.

I cough. "Er, by the way my Wi-Fi's a bit spotty today, can you hear me?"

"Yah! Yah, can you hear me?"

"Yah, yah, yah," I parrot back.

"Yah," she says again. "Your camera's a little shaky but I'm able to catch up to what you're saying…eventually."

With the Wi-Fi connection being a bit delayed, I realise I'm not pausing long enough to actually give Sammie a chance to respond. I'm going to have to learn to be okay with the long pauses today.

In case you haven't had your fill of creative darlings yet, Sammie is a comedian, writer, actor and, as a transwoman herself, is the founder of WE ARE TRANS, an organisation focused on spotlighting Trans voices in the Arts. One of their recent projects was a series of online standup shows called Every Body's Work, a fundraiser for Texas based abortion funds.

"I've been doing standup. *Lots* of standup. I've also been working with a non-profit theatre in New York on their non-discrudjda fkrhhhz fyshu wzer."

251

The spotty signal makes their speech unclear for a moment, and I feel it would be impolite to have Sammie repeat themselves, so I just say, "Oh...Nice!" Which I presume is true. Sammie *is* very nice. Though she's no pushover.

"I have a very low tolerance for bullshit! I'm in a relationship now that's coming up to three years and that will be the longest relationship I've been in." She narrows her eyes and drawls, "Usually, it's around six months and then I'm like, this is done."

I wonder whether it's just been down to finding the right person yet, but it's clear that after transitioning in their early twenties – nearly a decade ago – Sammie's learnt what she needs. "In adulthood it shifted from 'I don't feel comfortable with this' to, well after all that I've had to figure out about myself, and all that I've been through in my life, I have really strong boundaries. So, it's just like," she smiles again, but it's over the top in an irritated-customer-service-smile sort of way, "nope. Nope, nope, nope, you're done."

It was only after transitioning that Sammie was able to take a further look into their sexuality with fresh eyes. "It really started to dawn on me. I started to really accept being bi in adulthood and after that point I was like oh, I'm attracted to people of all genders and I start looking back at younger ages of myself and I'm just like," she draws in her breath and lets out a high-pitched, "OOOOoooooOOOOOOOH! So definitely some memories of being like, as young as eleven and looking back I'm like," she draws in a breath again and I turn the volume down on my laptop a couple of notches, "OoOOOooOOh! I had a CRUSH on you! That's what that whole thing was!"

When Sammie was younger and pretransition ("pretending to be a dude" as she puts it) her best friend was a boy who she'd spend all of her time with. They'd share punk music, watch lots of horror films and generally be nerdy loners together. She's not sure whether he knew that Sammie found him attractive, but Sammie became aware when changing in the boys' locker room for gym one day.

"I thought, 'Ron has *really* nice abs!' Wait, whyamIthinkingthat? Don't think that! So yeah. I definitely found him attractive."

As it became increasingly clear that she wasn't truly herself, the teenage Sammie found dating incredibly hard, whatever the gender of their desire. Physical intimacy was impossible. "As my younger self, I'd go on a date and I'd be like, nnnnoyeah I can't do this. I really couldn't *date* date. I hadn't come out. There was a girl at my school, we were really good friends. She asked me out and I got extremely awkward. I said," Sammie puts on a dull, deep tone, "'I'm not in a place where I can date right now.' That's what adults say when they're going through a divorce, sure, but it sounds WEIRD when a sixteen-year-old says it. But the thing is I was being honest! I was like, 'I can't.'"

Just prior to coming out, Sammie was sent to a support group for teenagers with severe depression. There she met a teenage girl called Lindsay who she dated for three months. Hiding all of her inner struggles, Sammie was incredibly numb and to this day can't be sure whether the attraction and connection to Lindsay was real or not. "I was so emotionally closed off and dissociative for so much of my childhood. But we were *both* very quiet, sad people. She'd call me like, 'Hey wanna go to the movies...?' and I'd say, 'Sure.' So, we got along great! She was great."

Sammie speaks urgently, recalling the breaking point, "It was at this time where it was all hitting me, 'I can't. I can't keep this inside anymore. When it finally hit me and I was like, 'Oh I can't keep pretending to be a *dude*' I just...broke up with her. I didn't tell her what was going on. I just...*broke up with her* and left her life."

"Did she take it badly?" I ask. Sammie's eyes widen. A teenage girl with depression getting ghosted before ghosting is even a known phrase?

"I mean...YAH."

"We'd been on a few dates. But I thought, 'are we even dating?' And this is so shitty because it was the budding of a relationship. So, some of these thoughts feel shitty to verbalise. But I thought, if this *was* real, I'd feel bad about this but really all I care about is that I've just got to get away! I don't know though, it was kind of real but it just wasn't at the time, y'know?"

As unique as Sammie's story is, I think we can all relate to the juvenile cowardice of first break ups.

"It's like I can't, how do I tell her this?! Oh, I know! I *won't* tell her this!" To demonstrate, Sammie gets up from her chair and physically runs away from the screen, calling out in a casual voice as if they're just popping out, "'Hey, this isn't working for me, we have to break up.'"

Now fully grown and on the other side of things, Sammie's thankfully not too hard on herself. It was a teenage love formed by two people in messed up places and wasn't reflective of either of their true selves. "That version of me that she found attractive wasn't me. She wouldn't like the real me anyway. And I'm not talking about the trans me but like, a completely different personality! A *happy* me!"

It's difficult to imagine Sammie as anything other than who she is now, but before coming out as trans she was in a perpetual state of numbness to survive. "I just seemed sad. And weird. Rather than openly and outwardly feminine. My parents were surprised when I came out, even though I was aware of it for a long time – but I was *really* good at hiding it. I don't know if they were ever *un*supportive but it took them a while to just wrap their heads around it, to figure out what that meant for the family dynamic. I have a brother and sister, both older than me. They were cool with it. But my parents? It took them a while just to get their heads around it."

In comparison, what was it liking coming out as bisexual? Sammie is out and proud in their standup and in everything they do.

255

"I came out as bi, probably to my brother and sister in maybe my late twenties. I didn't really make it the 'coming out' that trans was where I sat each person down and said, 'This is what's going on with me, I am trans.' It was really like in passive conversations like, 'Well yeah as a bi person...' or just like something will come on TV and I'm like, 'Oh you know I'm bi right? No? Eh, now you do.' Or I'd post it on FB and I'm like, 'Oh my dad will see that...Okay!'" (The bravest thing I've heard about Sammie yet is that she has her parents on Facebook.) Compared to the difficulty in their teens, Sammie truly does seem blasé about being bisexual. "I have a joke about this in my standup act. My presentation kind of runs the gamut. I dunno, I wear more menswear now than I did when I was pretending to be a dude, like suits and ties, 'cos I can do it the right way! Mom said, 'You know when you were growing up,'" she puts on a serious, quivering voice, "'We were prepared for gay...maybe we were prepared for woman...but we were never prepared for butch lesbian.' I said, 'Aww you've got nothing to worry about Mom, I'm bisexual.'"

Sammie transitioned a decade ago, aged twenty-three. "It was kind of like those dominoes started falling down as soon as I could say," Sammie declares triumphantly, "'I. AM. A WOMAN! And I guess that means I'm GAY!?'" It's such a declaration that I imagine it as a headline in a newspaper. It took roughly a couple of years of progress with her gender identity before Sammie could revisit her sexuality. It was an arrested development for a now twenty-five-year-old, but Sammie quickly realised that she found different sorts of people attractive.

We talk about online dating. Personally, I've always struggled with the apps. I met Harry when I saw him playing piano at a charity event and thought, "Yeah you're next." The guy before that I met while I was high on morphine in the hospital. That was pretty great. Ever thought you needed more confidence or to be better looking to talk to your crush? Nah mate, you need morphine.

Anyway, Sammie rather likes online dating – namely for getting all the labels out there in a non-invasive way.

"It was filled out right there on my *OkCupid* profile. So, it's all spelled out, being openly bi and trans. And that's been…over the years that's changed. There's definitely been earlier times where that label wasn't there, but it's always a conversation I've had to have. Now it's like, heeeere you go!

"There've been people I've been on dates with who have never found out about me being bi, especially early in my adult dating life where I myself was becoming more aware of it. And I was like, but 'I'm not bisexual though! I mean I find all genders attractive but…'" Sammie grins, shaking their hand, "And you know, *that's exactly what that means.* Early in my dating life I'm just going on dates with women and I thought, 'They don't need to know that I find other people attractive…do they?'"

Yet again the question arises. To tell or not to tell. Or when to tell. Does it matter or does it not? Sammie's journey has given her a lot of perspective. "Now I'm turning thirty-three next year, I realise it's a fundamental part of my identity. It's like yah, here ya go! Part of it's just about full acceptance of myself. For me, acceptance and claiming of my bisexuality is a piece of self-love. As long as it's safe to do so, I'm going to be open about things."

Sammie's found a sort of divergence in her attraction to different people. "My initial physical attraction type is like a small androgynous person in dapper clothing," she explains, before hooting appreciatively, "Woo hoo! Just, so many freaking butch women. But I've noticed that my *relationships* are with a fem. So, I'm very physically attracted to androgyny, but all the times I've had deep romantic attraction for someone, they've been femmes."

I think of some of the previously unavailable men I've chased like Mr Bojangles or the beautiful Italian nurse. I say, "I think plenty of people – whatever their sexuality – can definitely feel at times, 'Yep, I'm attracted to physical things that don't work out emotionally.'"

Sammie nods. "I like a bubbly personality, you know?! Long term, that is. Again, initially I like the quiet brooding person, I'm like, 'Yeah, they're cute.' But in a long-term relationship it's like *I* want to be the quiet brooding one!"

I bring up Steve's loose theory on his experiences with men being a sort of 'self-insertion' when infatuated with someone of the same gender, and that it's based on a lack of body confidence or identity crisis in himself. Sammie nods again. "Suddenly I'm becoming aware of crushes I had when I was younger. At times I look back when I'm like, "Oh no, no no, I wasn't attracted to her. I was *jealous* of her! But I was just like looking at her, feeling sad, feeling at a loss without her like, WHYYYY."

259

I go red in the face as I think of my own lesbian speed dating fiasco. 'Do I really like her, or do I just like her hair?'

Sammie's excited voice spills out over the screen, "I wonder the same thing now with an androgynous person in a suit! I have to stop myself and think, 'am I attracted to that person or do I just want to Rock. That. Suit?'"

"If a suit is questioning your sexuality then that must be a really nice suit."

Sammie's eyes widen. "Mmmhmmm."

The conversation leads back to the person Sammie's now with. "They're another transwoman. I've dated a trans man and been on dates with afab non-binary people, but this is my first time dating another transwoman."

I nod along to the Zoom camera while reaching for my phone off screen to google *afab*. For anyone as clueless as me, it means assigned female at birth. I thought she may have been describing their fabulous personalities.

"Maybe that's why this one is so much more successful than the other ones. We have a lot of shared experiences, shared interests but then also a lot of divergent interests that have sparked conversations. We're both huge nerds. And they knew I was bi from the first date."

I'm pleased to hear that Sammie's now happy in her personal life. I question if there's any difference in culture in the US that bisexuals face compared to the UK. Homophobia works differently in different countries, obviously. Even where it's not outlawed. But even in accepting or what you might call 'safe' spaces, there can be the same old story of bisexuals being greedy, obsessed with sex and more generally some scepticism. Sammie recalls those sceptics, "'Oh but are you REALLY bisexual?' A lot of, 'Yeeeeah but like, *are* you? You've only dated so-and-so type of person, so *are you?*' There's a lot of that." Sammie recalls telling a friend they were about to go on a date with someone, Suit Gal. Sammie offhandedly mentions that Suit Gal identifies as bisexual. This is before Sammie themself has come out as bisexual, and their friend interrupts her with a short but stern warning as if Sammie is reaching towards a hot kitchen hob rather than a sexy human.

"Oh, be *careful!*"

"What did they mean by 'be careful?'" I ask.

Sammie's eyes widen and she shrugs like a cartoon character. "I don't KNOW! Like unsafe physically?! Could this be a dangerous person? Or is this about the bi person being promiscuous? And the thing is, there is some – not to tread on anyone who calls themselves bisexual – but there can be some," Sammie takes a long pause to think of the right way to phrase the next part, "some people who use that word *incorrectly* just because they find trans people attractive. So, there is like, this warning from my friend could have been their concern for *me specifically.* 'Cos there are some people who are like," she puts on an obnoxious cheerleader voice, "'YAH! OKAY! I AM BISEXUAL. BECAUSE I DATE CIS WOMEN AND TRANSWOMEN.' And I'm just like yeah, er, that's a straight person. Not saying *all* straight people are the same in that feeling because I know they're not, but to me that is a spectrum of straight. In fact, that's straight and fetishizing. But this bisexual I was going to go on a date with wasn't like that, and I had only just come out as trans and my friend was like, 'Woah, woah, woah, *be careful.*' So, there is a little bit of that difficulty in it."

I saw a Drag Cabaret the other night. You'll be pleased to know that I did not go to see the same Drag King from Chapter One, no I went to seek out new victims. The show was called *Mulan Rouge* and it was a hybrid show of the tale of *Mulan* and Baz Luhrmann's *Moulin Rouge*, with the climax of the show resulting in Mulan saving the army by dancing to Pony, that famous stripper song from the *Magic Mike* film that Channing Tatum dances to. In short, it was absolutely fucking genius. And I fell completely in love with the person playing the Drag King version of Mulan, a transman. It's weird – I wonder why I'm drawn yet again to a beautiful person playing a Drag King. There's a masculinity there for sure, but you approach the person underneath the makeup in an almost gender-blind fashion. Maybe that's why I have a thing for them – maybe I like the freedom of

263

being gender-blind? Now that makes me panic. Have I been technically pancurious this whole time instead of bicurious? Am I actually just a spectrum of straight? Have I just been confused thanks to a couple of Drag Kings this whole time? (Fuck, maybe this is the evil Drag agenda those far-right people have been screaming about, it's not a creative expression of their identity at all, it's about how it makes ME ME ME feel!) I wonder what Sammie's thoughts are on the blurred lines between bisexual and pansexual. I tell her what I told Florian, that I fear that the use of the word bisexual could mean a non-binary erasure, or even just whether the term is now irrelevant. Looking at the word 'bi' it means two. I head to Google again for my research; Zain was right, it's the best place for 'research'. TikTok is too frantic. I google 'bi definition' and honestly all the definitions sound *very* sexy:

Two; having two. (Sounds like a dirty Shakespearean phrase) *Lasting for two.* (Er, two hours or two minutes?)

Twice over. (Front and back ehehehe.)

Denoting an acid salt. (Oh, STOP IT.)

I find Google's definition for bisexual:

sexually attracted not exclusively to people of one particular gender; attracted to both men and women.

Whomp WHOMP. 'Both.' Okay, so I guess by Google's definition, non-binary bisexuals don't exist.

Dear reader, you may think I'm maybe being oversensitive with this. The thing is, I know there are many battles to fight and I'm pretty sure in the grand scheme of life this isn't the worst thing that Google has ever done. (Especially when they're developing AI machines who are going fuck us all up in about twenty years. Or twenty seconds.) And the LGBTQ still have a lot of other life-threatening things to focus on. But still, this stuff does matter to people. Everyone knows that if Google reports something then it's true! And by 'everyone' I mean idiots who can't think for themselves (like meeee). But isn't the internet and apps all that we turn to now to grant us knowledge, wisdom and online shopping with next day delivery options? People tell you, 'I know about this, I've done my research.' They're not going to libraries or conducting interviews. They're not talking to people. They're on Google. Or TikTok. Or (insert latest thing here).

It's weird, isn't it? Online businesses are like the new empires. First there was the Roman Empire, now there is Amazon. Once there was Mansa Musa, now there is Google. They hold power. They're out there to please the user but they're still somehow exceptionally dictator-like.

Anyway, I do feel that anyone who is allied to bisexuals should pay attention to stuff like this. We can't expect people to understand the nuances of a bisexual identity and then completely disregard another person's nuanced identity. We'd look like idiots. Or maybe it's not erasure at all. Maybe it is the true definition of a bisexual? I recall Danni making a point of describing herself as a bisexual with 'genital preferences', or Florian and his adventures with either a Johnny Bravo or an Ariel.

Sammie reflects on an evolving LGBTQ community, as well as the rest of the world in a typical Sammie fashion. She shrugs and says, "I mean the term bisexual is what I use for me. And people say, 'Well actually you're pan.' But even if that's true, I like bisexual. And also, sorry to flag shame, but I like the flag more!"

I nearly choke on my cup of tea, Britishly.

"Sammie, you are the second person I've interviewed to say this. Whoever designed the bisexual flag? Mad props, your KPIs are through the roof."

Sammie laughs, "Look, even if I am pan, that's not the flag I'm bringing to the parade!"

Sammie sees the 'two' in the term bisexual in a different way. "Whereas pan I kind of use more to mean that like, gender isn't even a factor. And I know that just that separation is a little confusing. Does that make sense? It really is my view, it's more my definition. But just for the bisexual definition, there does seem to be a newer definition of bisexual, for the newer generation. We've kind of defined bisexual as still using the 'two' but it's," Sammie clears their throat, "I am attracted to people like myself and people unlike myself. I am attracted to people of my gender and to people not of my gender."

I love that. I love that so, so much that I think I'm going to pinch it for myself (that really is British of me). Sammie and I start wrapping up, and I ask if there's anything else they want to add.

Sammie's bright, expressive voice grounds itself. A lot of what is happening in the US right now hangs in the air. And dear reader, if you're reading this years from now and don't know what I'm talking about, then I hope to god that that's a good thing and that things worked out.

Sammie knows we're stronger together when fighting for human rights, but they want that to be reflected within the community more. "There's a large amount of infighting in the bisexual community which I wish we could do away with. Am I bi enough? Are you bi enough? Oh, you're not bi actually you're describing being pan. Or queer. And it's like," she pinches the bridge of her nose, fatigued, "Look. Let people – as long as they're not using a shitty definition like the one I used earlier for that fetishizing person – just let people define themselves. Stop orientation policing people."

Sammie's right. I think how you identify within yourself matters more than what people can see on the outside. And what's within me? I told you, dear reader, that my story stopped at chapter one, but I don't think it ever did. I'm not just interviewing bi people, I'm interviewing people in my life that happen to be bi. So many of them were friends or have become friends. So many put their trust in me as they told their story. Sammie makes me realise I've been closed off, not to them but to myself. I've always felt protective and allied to the human rights and human stories of the LGBTQ, but never like I was experienced enough to plant my flag down. *I've just not clocked in the hours.* But I've found so much in common with many of the people I've interviewed. The only thing that ever stopped me was myself, not my lack of interest. In fact, the more I think about it, the more bicurious sounds like it doesn't fit me at all. Because I haven't been curious, have I? I've stayed away. If anything, I'm an incurious bisexual.

"And we all deal with it," Sammie says, "It's in the culture. I'm not gonna say it's impossible…but it's really hard to escape without queerphobia and biphobia touching you and affecting you. The relationship before this current one was a great guy, it was my first time dating another trans person and my first time dating a guy so I felt like a"—she does air quotes and rolls her eyes at herself—"real bisexual! OOOoooOoh!"

Anyway, Sammie and I stop stalling and wrap up for real this time. I tell Sammie a little bit more about this book, how I'm interviewing different people.

"You know, you're the only non-British person I reckon I'm speaking to for this book," I say. "You're special."

"OoooOoooh!"

"Yeah, I was like, 'fuck yeah, I'm gonna have a Yank!'"

Sammie smiles, but it's that customer service smile I've seen before. "Sure! Yah! I mean, we, we don't call ourselves that." And just like that, I've made myself feel awkward again. But it's alright. I say my goodbyes like how I drink shots of tequila at a Mulan/Moulin Rouge Drag Cabaret Night – I do about ten billion of them before abruptly calling it a night.

"Bye, bye, bye, bye bye by byebyebyby!"

But not Sammie. In one quick swoop of a button and a cheery farewell, The Demon Lady Lord of The Damned disappears. I close the laptop lid, my mind racing. I feel like I started out these interviews like I know how my own story ended, now I'm second guessing myself (I really thought I was done overthinking). All this time I've been gatekeeping myself about an identity that really is no one else's to define but mine. Fuck it, dear reader. I've got more in me than just curiosity.

I'm bisexual.

HARRY AND THOMASIN

The most open I ever saw Harry be about his bisexuality was a year ago at a party. My friend Liam was hosting a get-together, and a friend of his called Carrie, who Harry and I had only just met that night, was talking about changing her dating app for the first time to include women as well as men. I can't remember what he said exactly, but Liam started cracking jokes about her being bisexual, which Carrie did not take well. She told Liam off and Liam – who had not meant any harm but at this stage was too tipsy to recover the conversation – tried to defend himself rather than apologise. I know Liam and I know he was being honest when he said this, but it came across as flippant, "It's not a big deal."

Carrie complained how it *was* a big deal for her to even tell us and that she really wasn't ready to laugh about it. It ended with a tense silence. Harry, who had been pretty quiet all evening, suddenly said, "If it makes anyone feel any better, I've sucked cock."

I feel that usually a sentence like that would open up the floor to chaos at a party, but in this case, it diffused the situation. Carrie scoffed but immediately eased up, and Liam, who was already pouring shots, declared a toast to sucking cock. Essentially, Harry came out that night not to cause a fuss but out of sheer politeness. The perfect party guest!

I later talk to Harry that night in bed. I remember our first date well. About three hours in we go to get pizza, and over food he gently asks whether I'm bisexual. He's seen some of my standup online where I briefly allude to it. I immediately feel defensive, hoping this date isn't about to sour.

"Why do you want to know?" I smile tightly.

Cutting up his pizza with his knife and fork (because it's our first date) he barely looks up, saying casually, "Oh, it's just, well, me too."

Back in the present, I ask him more about it. He's been on his own journey, which isn't to be shared here, but he's seen straight men explore their bicuriousity without labelling it as such. "I think any guy is bi as long as a girl is involved in some way. I think that's at the centre of what allows most men to be bicurious. They get to secretly enjoy all these things under the guise of tolerance because there's a girl there to bond over. I think guys get very horny over the idea of bonding over their love of girls. They like to secretly sexualise it. And I think a lot of straight men explore bisexuality because it's a dominance, a power play. The kink of exploring that taboo – especially if they're maybe not into it

– that is the line some men go to. They want to resist it and that itself is the thrill." The way he describes it, it sounds like straight men's exploration of bisexuality reinforces their masculinity, maybe in the same way girls drunkenly snogging on nights out reinforces a certain feminine experience. The thrill, the frivolity, the way it leads back to heterosexuality in the end. Harry doesn't appear to have any feelings on it, but he's adamant it's another valid experience of bisexuality, even if it is momentary. "They wouldn't go around describing themselves as a Betty Both Ways."

"Is that what we're calling me now?"

So, I've always been an open book with Harry, even when I'm still trying to write it. He knows about my recent revelation, and he wants to help me. We're not exactly Ros and Luke, but we discuss the idea of exploring our sexuality through other means. Together. Call me crazy, but after all these stories I'm feeling emboldened. Maybe you are too? That or bloody horrified.

Harry tells me about a place that he's heard of called Brazil. It's a naturist spa in London that has private rooms for *play*. Unlike most naturist spas, there's not a clear-cut division between being naked and natural and being naked and sexyyyyy. People are heavy petting in steam rooms and they're also getting a nice little detox treat. Swingers go and it could be a good opportunity to meet open-minded, like-minded people like ourselves to...ahem...give roses that were originally gifted from work to. Veronica's story served as a warning; I'm very aware that it could complicate things and that the idea of it is more sexy than the reality. And Andrew's story of the gay sauna sounds full-on. But still, we take a peek at the website.

The website looks like it was made in 2002. It has about eighty-seven different fonts and has made liberal use of the old Microsoft WordArt. In a sunny comic sans they have the text,

Bring Your Own Booze!

In a serious Times New Roman they write,

Abuse towards our staff will not be tolerated.

And then the terms and conditions are in windings.

They also have a **Bring Your Own Food** rule, which is even stranger to me. Am I allowed to eat Tuc biscuits in the sauna? If so, hold the sex that's all I care about experiencing, that sounds euphoric. And what's to stop me rocking up with a full Sunday Roast in some Tupperware?

We head there on a Monday evening and I'm not joking, dear reader, I am the ONLY BLOODY WOMAN there. (Bloody as in 'damn it' not that it's my time of the month, just to be clear. Maybe that is clear. What's wrong with me?) I walk through the doors in my towel and feel a million eyes on me from a plethora of guys that I don't feel any particular attraction to. So, no luck for me and certainly no luck for those blokes. Harry and I end up in the relax space, scoffing our Tuc biscuits on a sunlounger while enjoying an old Superman movie on their giant TV, and the staff are very welcoming. It actually ends up feeling kind of cosy. The spa is also not bad. I wear a swimsuit, so I don't feel too self-conscious, and Harry wedges himself between me and anyone playing a one-way game of footsie in the hot tubs. It's a weird vibe and we laugh about it the whole way back, but we somehow end up going again on a Saturday night. Saturdays are couples only and the atmosphere is a lot more lively and a lot less *desperately sad*. It's even sort of sexy. You know, in between the Tuc biscuits and strange men. We end up going a few more times, sporadically, just to enjoy the facilities and atmosphere as a couple, do a load of sexy eye contact (gasp!) at the odd pair of hotties and keep more or less to ourselves. To be honest, dear reader, I have no idea where I'm going with this story about Brazil other than to tell you these are the lengths that I've gone to in order to try and explore my bisexuality within a monogamous relationship. And to leave you with one final confession.

"I'd never want you to feel like you've missed out on anything by being with me."

That's what Harry tells me. But I really don't feel that way and I never did. I think I've learnt from these interviews that I don't need to do anything physical in order to validate that part of me. And besides, maybe I will act on it, or maybe I won't. Truth be told, I think I'll well and truly be out of the closet once this thing gets published. Part of me is hoping this book tanks so I don't have to face that (so don't feel too bad if you give it a terrible review). Part of me is hoping that the publisher turns out to be some kind of scam artist and this isn't in fact a real book deal at all, and it will never see the light of day. (Sorry to my editor Enda for saying that – and also sorry for encouraging readers to give it a terrible review.) And then there's the huge part of my heart that hopes you've enjoyed the ride, dear reader. And maybe anyone reading who has had similar internal struggles even shuts the book feeling a bit less alone in that. Maybe even feeling some pride or acceptance. Just know that those things aren't necessarily a station you arrive at and then the journey is complete, but rather a plate you have to continually spin. I'll still be spinning my own plate over here, even when you finish this book.

I wish I had a better conclusion for you, but I don't feel articulate enough to get into the nitty gritty of what this really means for me going forward. I hide behind jokes and cartoons instead.

The potential to act on it though is there, and it is exciting. And mine. As much as I feel like I've spilt my guts in this book, I think that (for now) I'll keep my own future adventures off the page. I mean, I've got to keep some things to myself, haven't I? I've got to protect Harry too (and Carol if you're still reading up to this point then I'm not talking about your son Harry, I'm talking about Prince Harry; I have a new job as his ghostwriter, and this is actually his sequel to *Spare*). If I'm being completely pragmatic though, I'm sure to you, dear reader, this book is nothing that will sit in your mind for too long. We devour so much content, so many words that what's another confession about sexuality to you? Not much at all. You can find a million strangers yelling in caps lock or hollering into their microphones about much more personal things on social media – maybe it's even distracted you from finishing this book (it certainly stopped me writing it). But you're a stranger to me and I'm putting it out there to you and the rest of the world, and that's a little scary. And if you're *not* a stranger, well then that's even scarier. Nan, if you're reading this, JESUS CHRIST, I TOLD YOU NOT TO READ IT THE TITLE WAS A JOKE WHAT HAVE YOU DONE!!!

But bloody hell if it isn't obvious by now, then I am definitely, definitely, *definitely* bi.

ACKNOWLEDGEMENTS

I owe all the gratitude I have to the people who let me tell their story. Your bravery, humility and perspectives have not only been the heart of this book but they have helped me infinitely with my own journey. Thank you.

A huge thank you to my editor Enda Kenneally for guiding me through this process and for believing in my vision. I'm sorry that I'm still useless with working Microsoft word. Troy Hewitt, you took a chance on this concept when it was little more than a few sentences long. Thank you to Vulpine Press for giving me a platform I never thought I'd get.

Thank you to Luka for helping bring my illustrations into the 21st century! While I was still drawing cartoons on napkins you were busy training in graphic design.

Thank you to my wonderful partner 'Harry' who has never stopped encouraging me throughout this whole thing, and to all my friends who have kept me focused. Amy especially.

I'd also like to thank my Year 6 English teacher Mr Hocking and my Year 9 teacher Mr Wolfe. I'm sorry that I can't remember your first names but teachers make all the difference in the world. You really made me believe I could write. And thank you to Johnny Neal who ignited that writing passion back in me when I was in my twenties.

Finally, dear reader, if you're still reading this far, thank you for taking a chance on this book out of your many, many options! I am very lucky indeed.

Thomasin is a writer, comedian and actor in London.
Find her on TikTok and Instagram @thomasinlockwood